THE
SYSTEM

ROD MARSDEN

Prime Seven Media
518 Landmann St.
Tomah City, WI 54660

Printed in the United States of America

To a place long ago with family, a Holden station wagon, a fishing rod and a Daredevil comic book. It was during one of those glorious May holidays. We parked close to the Clarence River, near Maclean, the most Scottish town in New South Wales, Australia. There was no pressure, no pain, just a day that ended slowly and was then missed by all there with me in that twilight of being young. In later years, my youngest sister settled in Maclean and raised a family there.

To Rosalind of Padstow Heights, New South Wales, my first love.

In memory of Don Boyd, an Australian science fiction writer and friend.

To Kathy, who has remained friends with me and to Kim and Debra, my two charming sisters.

To Lyn McConchie for her advice.

Table of Contents

CHAPTER ONE

None but the Brave

A form of happiness of a sort, at last, thought Ross. I've beaten the system, or Glenda Evens, my lady love, has done it for me. Did we do it together? All those reasons concocted by society to keep me alone are now gone forever!

He looked around his modest home, south of Wollongong. He had his books, DVDs, and photos. He touched them, took them down, and stroked them like a cat. In doing so, the books and DVDs evoked memories of where they were purchased and why. The photos captured moments in time and space that had helped heal him and bring him back to a sense of being part of the real world.

Glenda had her books and DVDs. She also took them down, dusted them, and returned them where they belonged. Was she more practical than he was? He thought so. Still, she had memories she was happy to share with him of the time they were not together. Family back then, and when they were together, was essential to who she was and who she might become.

They had an unusual coffee table made of polished oak with a top designed especially for them. It held coins and bills worldwide on soft, green velvet, covered by special glass. Ross had seen something similar in Hawaii decades ago and wanted to create his version. The idea charmed his lady love, so it was made.

Among the coins were those brought to Australia by his grandfather after the First World War. Some were from Egypt, and others from France. He added Australian coins with special meaning, like the one-dollar piece fashioned in memory of the dancing man who did his thing to celebrate the end of the Second World War. Glenda provided notes from the USA, Canada, and the UK. In terms of money, the twentieth and early twenty-first Centuries were laid out for visitors and themselves. It was the more practical world they barely belonged to. It was disappearing because of the bank card.

He recalled a documentary on the English white notes that had to be replaced because they were such a forger's dream. He thought it would have been nice to have had one of those as part of their collection. Glenda, the woman he cared most for, agreed. The more modern English twenty-pounder was impressive. It had protective devices, much like modern Australian notes.

Ross also thought it would have been nice to have Confederate money from the American Civil War, but that was also hard to come by.

Making lots of money had never been the goal for either of them. There were no regrets about this, though Ross sometimes wondered what his life would have been like if he had been born into wealth or had a better head for business. Either way, his outlook would have been different, as would how his life had played out.

There were stories about idiots who became wealthy because of the lottery and ended up owing millions. Ross knew that wouldn't have happened to him or Glenda if they had won big. Still, it was surprising how many people keen on wealth had no idea what to do with it when they got it. There was a story about some fool who bought dozens of four-wheel drives and spent the rest of a million on champagne, beer, and prostitutes. It was all gone in a month, and even selling the cars didn't help much. Whatever he got back on the sales, he swiftly went through and cried for more capital to spend.

Ross imagined that those who succeeded in winning big on the lottery or some other game of chance shunned publicity, which was why they did all right. It seemed to him that every second person believed that money could not buy happiness. He wasn't one of them. To him, it was a case of what could be done and what should be done with a windfall.

"It is what you do with your money that counts," he once told his lady love over breakfast one morning. "Not having to be tight with it must be stupendous, not that we're ever that tight. I remember a soap ad on TV where a wealthy couple jetted around the world while luxuriating in a bathtub onboard their plane. Not something I would do in a jet, just in case of turbulence, but jetting wherever you would like to go would be fantastic."

Ross also envisioned a publishing empire and the ability to acquire the latest photographic equipment and renowned paintings by celebrated artists such as Gene Colan. Additionally, he imagined purchasing houses in various parts of Australia while ensuring that doing so doesn't send even a millionaire, or possibly a billionaire, broke. Ah! But it was all just a daydream! His chances of becoming rich were so small that it was laughable. He was satisfied with what he had, and so was Glenda.

Once they had moved in together, Glenda introduced Ross to better coffee, biscuits, and yogurt. He recalled a time in the 1960s when only young women and those recently arrived from Europe ate yogurt. For the young women, it was to stay slim and attractive, as the TV ads implied. A few decades later, Ross ate yogurt because it was cheap. He also had to have something for lunch.

Once they got together, Ross and Glenda could afford a bigger television screen and more comfy seating in the lounge room. Thanks to her, he saw more live theatre and had weekends away that genuinely made life worth living.

The inside walls of their home were light blue like a summer sky, and the artwork they contained belonged to both. A bird here, a view of a temple in Bali there. The bedroom had two beds, and when they felt like it, they bounced from one to the other and back again, like he imagined twenty-something kids doing. He was never like that at twenty-something, but he had wanted to be. Their home had large windows, which let in plenty of light.

Ross Martin was enthralled by how everything he had ever wanted finally came his way. The system had been so brutal and unrelenting. He had taken shelter from it in books and DVDS. Now, thanks to her, he no longer needs to do so. Photography was better for him and remained so. It made him an explorer, and he knew that was something she could admire about him.

This was a house he could not have afforded without her. They both had units when they met. They pooled their finances and purchased a property near the beach. On nights in summer, they sat outside on their verandah and listened to the waves moving up and down the nearby beach.

Ross was dumpy and short. The dumpiness stemmed from years spent behind a computer, a lack of exercise, and an unhealthy diet. The lack of hair was due to old age. The glasses had been there ever since he could no longer afford contacts. He had a round face, blue eyes, and a smile he hadn't worn in decades until he met her.

He looked at the woman who had come into his life close to the end of it and wondered how that had happened. Why was he blessed now of all times? It didn't make much sense until he realised neither of them had anything to lose by coming together and everything to gain. Was this the only way he could ever beat the system?

Her hair was silver, whereas it once had been black, like a raven's feather. Where he had hair on top of his head, it was thinning and grey. His beard was the same colour as the hair on his head. She told him it tickled her when they kissed.

The song *You and Me Against the World* came to him. Paul Williams sang it way back in the 1970s. Others saw it as a song sung to a child. Ross always envisioned it as defiance against the system. Finding the other person, he knew, was the near impossible part, yet, close to the conclusion of his life, he saw her, and they could be defiant together.

There was courage now, but not as much was at stake as before. Fear had been conquered at last, and it had taken decades for this to happen. Had she also been afraid when she was younger? There would have been no reason to believe so in the decades he had lived through, but he knew he could be wrong.

Ross remembered the holidays he took up north with his parents. They had retired to a small fishing village and lived near a forest. The river, beaches, and a headland were nearby.

Every morning, his mother would go to her front yard and feed the birds with seed and bread dipped in honey water. She would have him feed them some mornings when he was on holiday with them, which he enjoyed. He would call out none but the brave as he distributed the food. He then stood still, daring the birds to come to him and take what he wanted to give them. They took courage to do so since he was so much bigger than they were.

The little green lorikeets tended to be braver than the slightly larger rainbow lorikeets, so size didn't always come into the equation. Bravery might have something to do with who was hungrier. This revelation would follow Ross back to his working life. If you want something bad enough and are a bird, you will risk it all to get it. Could that also be true of people?

On one of his holidays to where his parents had retired, he was fishing the river at night when he spotted a little white owl perched on a branch, not a foot away from him. He had this owl as his companion for two hours while he fished. It was undoubtedly doing its fishing, but why sit so close to him? Didn't it fear what he might do? This was not the case. Somehow, it had worked out; he would do it no harm, and they could fish together. *Is this a different kind of courage?* Ross wondered. This incident would stay with him.

Glenda, the woman he was now with, asked him if he had time for ham and eggs before he ventured out to take wildlife photos. He told her yes. They took turns making breakfast, and he liked it. His specialty was French toast, which she loved. It was such a good relationship that it would have been impossible decades ago.

Ross understood that when he worked for the government in an office in the 1990s, the price he would pay for asking an office woman out if she didn't want to go out with him was high. He once had visions of having his hands tied behind his back while standing on a chair with a rope around his neck. In saying yes, the woman would untie him, remove the rope, and go to a place of wonder with him. The woman, in saying no, would then kick the chair out from under him and leave him to hang by the neck until he was dead.

The reality was that a no could cost him the job he needed to keep. Even a yes might have its hazards. What if he went out with her and she didn't like his company? Could that also result in an end to a promising career? He didn't know. In ten years, he had not dared; he had not ventured to find out. Others did so, and their boldness was rewarded. He wondered about that. Was the possible date with some woman worth risking everything? And why should it be so in the first place? There were those guys who left work without a word as to why. Could they have been the ones who failed and lost everything because of a woman in the office?

What, then, is so wrong with asking someone if they want to get coffee with me after work? And not asking multiple times, just once. If yes, we move on. If not, that should be the end of it. Where was the complication and the insult in being asked?

Working for the government had its fragile moments. Ross recalled an incident that still angered him even after all this time. He was expected to teach this young woman how to use a new computer system. He sat close to her on the computer to show her, and there lay the problem. According to her, he sat too close. His answer to the inquiry was straightforward. If he showed anyone the new system, he would sit near them. It didn't matter what gender or age.

He didn't even like the looks of that young woman and didn't want her company. He didn't mind her chubbiness. What he didn't like most was her attitude. Later, through another office woman, he discovered that she had a terrible older relative whom he resembled. What this relative had done to her, he didn't know, nor did he care to find out. It was all too creepy, and he was happy when he moved away from her to another section.

Ross's sister, Kate, once told him of awful men who chased her around the office where she was employed. This was before she took up a position with a tyre company and was working better hours and with better people. Hence, there was genuine sexual harassment that had to be done away with. He agreed to that. He didn't want anyone to be harassed by anyone else, especially his sister. He never cared to be accused of something he hadn't done nor intended to do.

As he dug into breakfast, Ross sometimes wondered if this life was better than he deserved. There were times, long ago, when he didn't have breakfast and settled instead for a biscuit and a cup of coffee.

Ross recalled how a slightly older office woman, who was so tall her breasts were at eye level to Ross, presented him with difficulties. She was liberated and never wore a bra; she jiggled as she walked. Moving past her to get to his work cubicle, he didn't know where to look. Straight ahead was no good because of the breast movement. Craning his neck to her eye level, he felt it made him look unnatural, and he was likely to bump into a wall. Looking down was subservient, and he didn't like that at all, but maybe she did. She wore slinky tops and miniskirts. Was she a Madam Whiplash groupie? Madam Whiplash is an Australian television personality of the 1970s.

Maybe her snarl was a come-on. If so, it was cringeworthy. He wanted no part of her twisted fantasies! Could it have been the start, in her head, of a Helen Reddy I Am Woman roar? A triumphant lioness thing? Yes, she always had a scowl, as if he had done something wrong and continued doing it. He noticed she acted the same way with other office guys who were shorter than her. Was she looking for a naughty boy? Was that it? Well, it wasn't going to be him! He had more dignity than that!

I'm only human! With a sigh, he thought about what he saw at eye level and her reactions to his seeing. He never said a word, and she never said anything to him, and they both kept it that way for a couple of months. And then she was gone, probably to bigger and better opportunities. He read somewhere that Mickey Rooney, the short actor, always preferred women much taller than himself. Ross wondered why.

In college, Ross encountered a towering woman who became interested in him. He found this out from another college student too late. He wondered if that lofty woman would have been suitable for him if he had taken a chance on her. Could she have been good for him if he had been smarter? Could that office woman's glare and possible kinky head trip have followed him to college?

Decades after leaving college, Ross did some writing for a local theatre company and came upon a genuine Madame Whiplash type and her wimpy male companion. He was far from impressed with both of them. The wimpy one, no doubt, had gone from women being equal to men to women being superior. No way was Ross willing to go there, even on a bet!

The wimpy guy got jealous of Ross and put a half-filled coffee container atop Ross's backpack when Ross wasn't looking. When Ross arrived at the train station for his trip home, he came upon the container and the mess it had made, including an old book from his backpack that his sister had given him ages ago. *There is something wrong with anyone who acts that way,* Ross thought. *Suppose the twit wants to be subjugated, fine. But leave my books, backpacks, and me out of it!*

There was a young blonde theatre woman who got her wires crossed when it came to Ross. Names didn't mean much to him, so he thought nothing of using a name like hers in a play he wrote. Thus, she felt he was attracted to her, which led to awkward moments. She looked funny at him and snubbed him. He tried to talk to her soon after he understood she had that notion in her head, but couldn't find a quiet moment with her to do it, and he figured it probably wouldn't do any good anyway. She was as washed-out white as a silvery fish caught on a hook. Being so pale, she would have done well for herself in medieval Europe. In modern Australia, she couldn't be so grand, and she would have to suffer sunburn in summer. He was happy to be her friend, and when that wasn't working out, he wanted nothing more to do with her. He decided he didn't need her and tried to keep his distance. Let her believe she was a sex pot when she was no such thing.

There were also Snags about (Sensitive New Age Guys) in the office and elsewhere where he had been previously employed. He suspected women were happy to go out with them and to treat them like girlfriends, but that was it. He could never imagine any woman marrying a Snag, so Ross had no intentions of becoming one. Was he one now, he wondered? No. He sometimes had arguments with the woman he was content to end his life with. A Snag would agree to everything she said; that was not how Ross ever wanted to live.

A peculiar incident occurred while he worked at that government office, which stayed with him. A friend was accused of sexually harassing this young woman. She was interviewed. The harassment stemmed from his failure to ask her out. She expected him to do so because she was attracted to him, and he was harassing her by not doing so. It took no time for those sitting in judgment to dismiss her claim. After that, no man was willing to be in her company for fear that she would try it on with him. She was let go. Ross thought she was attractive enough, but he wanted nothing to do with a woman that crazy. He could imagine her loving him, turning on him, and then wondering why he didn't love her anymore. *Melodrama is for the stage*, Ross thought. *Those who want to live anxious lives are welcome to it, but that's not me!*

For a couple of years, Ross was friends with a lesbian. He felt safe with her because they both understood that their relationship was just a friendship, nothing more. "We're just friends," she told him one day. "Don't expect more than that."

"I won't," replied Ross, feeling calm and somehow assured this relationship wouldn't blow up in his face.

She claimed to have been a male Indian warrior in a past life. Hence, she was interested in the Indian Wars that erupted after the American Civil War. Ross was fascinated by the American Civil War.

There was no fuss, no bother, no sex politics. It didn't matter that she wasn't good-looking since Ross knew that even a not-so-pretty woman could foul things up for him if she wanted to. Not all women were like that, but enough were to be cautious. This woman just needed a friend, and that was fine with him.

Ross was moved to the publications section, an all-male area. The leader was Sid, a robust fellow and a former football player, keen on team building. He took people who were rejected from other places and turned them into hardworking, dedicated team members. Other leaders didn't appreciate what he was able to do. It reflected poorly on them that they were incapable of being like Sid.

Ross enjoyed his time in publications. Then, a woman from South America joined Sid's group. Ross thought she would be trouble, but she was friendly and happy instead. He found her excellent company. She spoke about her family and her origins. He discovered there was more than one type of corn on the cob. And so, publications continued to be good for him.

Some afternoons after leaving the office, he was on the train going home and thought of approaching a woman on board, but never did. It just felt wrong. He wouldn't have wanted to be bothered by a stranger at that time of day, so he thought it was amiss to do so to someone else.

After the publications section relocated to Canberra, Ross was assigned to an accounts section where an elderly and challenging woman of Japanese descent was in charge. She had grown up in Imperial Japan and carried with her, from her youth, a sense of which races had value and thus importance and which races had very little worth and, therefore, very little meaning to their existence. She thought of the Chinese as being rubbish and verbally abused workers of Chinese descent. "You drop a coin and see them all scramble for it!" cried this woman one day. "They have no integrity at all. They are nothing."

She considered male Islanders to be monkeys in suits. "They are dumb as bricks, nothing more," she once told Ross. She had an even lower regard for Islander women.

There was an Islander gentleman who hated doing business with her so much that he would only interact with Ross. He would wait until she left her station before chatting with him. The Islander was mild, thoughtful, and nonconfrontational for a big guy. Ross knew he would have no problem breaking the Japanese woman in two, but preferred keeping out of her way. Neither he nor Ross fully understood her, nor did they want to if it meant becoming like her.

This Japanese woman talked too much about what she thought of others to the point where Ross would have happily wrung her scrawny neck. Some of the workers of Chinese descent came to think of him as being on her side, and he had to convince them he had to work with her, so he kept his mouth shut and got on with whatever he needed to get on with. The one time he tried to shut her verbal abuse down, she came at him with her nasty tongue, and that lasted two whole weeks.

There came a day when he got so frustrated with her and her lack of respect for himself and others that he snapped a pen in front of her. She reported him. He put his case to the big bosses, who turned out to be so into politically correct office politics that they feared her. They didn't demote him but moved him away from her. For this, he was grateful.

Keeping this Japanese woman the way she was, Ross saw reverse racism, which was popular in offices in the 1990s. He was not good because he was male and white. Had there been racists of the past who looked like him? Possibly. But he felt he should be given the benefit of the doubt, just like anyone else. Was this part of the system out to break him? He thought so, and, in that office, it came very close to doing so. He became ill with the injustice of it all, and when retrenchment was offered, he took it to get out from under. No doubt, the Japanese woman always thought she was in the right because no one above her was ever willing to tell her she was wrong.

Thanks to ten years working in such an environment, Ross felt paralysed, with no ability whatsoever to form any relationship with the opposite sex other than friendship. In his mind, he built this barrier to protect himself from what he considered the system. It took an extraordinary woman to help him dismantle it. Looking at her across the table at breakfast, he had to wonder why she did it for him.

Decades earlier, Ross's brother, Ian, got a young woman pregnant. They had a girl out of wedlock and then got married. The score in the end was two girls over five years. Additionally, Ross's sister, Kate, married a man named Arnold, and they had two girls and a boy. Ross never really understood why the system had allowed any of that to happen, just that it did. He was glad for his sister because he figured she deserved every happiness. It took a while before he could be delighted for his brother.

Ross met the woman he would love for the rest of his life, but it was too late for her to have children or for him to become a father. He had to wonder what he had missed out on and why.

Ian was stockier than Ross when Ross was as skinny as a weed. Maybe this stockiness meant something, or Ian, being a bad boy rather than a good fellow, was the thing women most admired for some weird reason. Ross's father once told Ross that Ian would have turned out stronger than him if not for an earlier attack of scarlet fever. This did not make Ross feel at all good about his younger brother. For years, it had created a sense of animosity between them that shouldn't have been there. It was also another reason why Ross couldn't see taking up sports as a good option. If he was meant to be physically less than his brother, that side of life wasn't for him. Ross's father should have known better.

As for being wrong, as a teenager, Ian once chucked rocks down onto traffic from an overhead bridge. No one was killed, but even so, the police were not impressed. Ross's father had to collect him from the police station. On another occasion, he stole a car and took it for a high-speed joy ride. The car ended up in a ditch and out of petrol. The police made an easy grab. He only just squeezed out of that one without jail time. He would have gone to lockup if he had been a little older. In the end, Ross was glad it hadn't happened to his brother. His dad paid for any damages to the car, which also helped.

Ian could have had more courage and stupidity than Ross, which made a difference in their lives. Ross never got along with Susan, Ian's woman. In part, it was Ross's envy of his brother. It was something that didn't hold up very well after his brother got sick from drug taking and could only do part-time work. Being a bad boy had caught up with him. There was a time, months before this sickness, when Ian made the best effort to get along with his brother. They went fishing together. When Ian's first daughter turned twenty-one, Ross sent her a present. It was a necklace with colourful metal butterflies. After that, Ross loses contact with Ian and his brood completely. He wondered if that was for the best.

Ian was skilled at copying the work of certain cartoonists, but he has yet to develop his style, which would make him a true artist and earn him a living. Could he have made it big with pen, paper, and ink if he had put his mind to it? Ross thought that was possible, but Ian needed more discipline to make it happen. Yet he managed to get the girl without discipline and sired children with her, so discipline wasn't everything.

Ross felt Ian could have made more out of his life if only someone had shown him how. But there was no one around to do it. Their father did what he could, but knew nothing about art. Their mother also didn't know enough to be of help. Ross could also say that, for decades, the same was true of himself if the notion of art could extend to writing and photography. Ross had given Ian a couple of books on drawing, but didn't know if he had looked at them. He hoped he had and that Ian had made a better go at art than he thought he had done.

It was Ross's understanding that studying how great artists managed their art was how many famous artists began their journey. He also understood that an artist had to be dedicated to drawing for years before achieving commercial success. He doubted Ian had it in him to get there, but he had hoped, in old age, he was wrong. He had lost contact with his brother, so there was the possibility that Ian had had some minor success as an artist. Additionally, Australia was not a particularly favourable environment for artists in general.

The good boy bit was always with Ross, and he didn't like it. His dad thought he was a good boy, and so did his mother. There was no comment from his sister Kate, who didn't seem to care about good or bad when it came to her brothers. The good boy bit had turned Penelope, a woman he was keen on in college, into just a friend. Things might have been different if he had been someone like the Fonz out of Happy Days, but that would never have been him. He would have loved to snap his fingers and have young women suddenly appear.

Now, with the woman he loved, it no longer mattered. He was just himself, whatever that might mean. With her help, he had beaten the system that, for many years, had subjugated him and made the bad guy, in his eyes, supreme.

CHAPTER TWO

Defying Logic

For decades, Ross Martin made the mistake of always trying to be a reasonable fellow. There were times when being reasonable or logical didn't work. Time and time again, he saw irritatingly illogical people gain ground. Sometimes, it had to do with religion, and at other times, it had to do with communism, political correctness, or woke. Was the system involved in the illogic? He thought so.

He recalled how, early in the 21ˢᵗ Century, someone had decided, despite much evidence to the contrary, that Cleopatra was black. Why couldn't she remain of Macedonian heritage like many scholars agreed upon? There was a well-known bust of Cleopatra, and she did indeed look Macedonian. Why mess up history for point scoring? It didn't make sense.

Going back to his childhood, Ross remembered how Christian preachers of every denomination pushed the notion of no sex before marriage. For most people living in the 20ᵗʰ and 21st Centuries, this didn't work for them at all. It certainly didn't seem to apply to his brother. If Christianity, in general, could enforce the no sex before marriage rules with imprisonment or worse for those who disobeyed, Ross reckoned the result would be the end of Christianity.

Ross knew of a pope who not only had a mistress but also children, even though he should have been celibate. What's more, he was one of the better popes!

He remembered a communist art teacher who did not doubt that communism was the way forward for everyone. She couldn't be persuaded otherwise, even after the Cold War had ended. She did, however, think it not right that a writer, Salman Rushdie, be given a death sentence by Muslim fanatics, and in this, he was in agreement with her.

Salman Rushdie's book, *The Satanic Verses*, when it first came out, was banned from sale in the UK for fear of Muslims there rioting. Clever booksellers sold a less popular novel and threw in The Satanic Verses for free, thus getting around that ruling. There was no such ban in Australia. Ross bought the art teacher a copy of the book as a birthday gift. She told him that every such book sold was a raised fist to freedom against oppressive, illogical religious nutters. Years later, a friend told him the book was poorly written and might have never been popular without the illogical death sentence thus the nutters had defeated themselves.

From his early years onwards, he hated bullies and, over time, he could not see Muslim fanatics as being more than bullies with fake religious power.

Ross Martin wondered why Spock's logic in the Woke television show had to be wiped out. Was nothing sacred to those who made that show? He gathered from what they said about themselves that they thought they had the right to do what they did.

So, throw away Spock's logic and still have Star Trek? That, to Ross, made no sense at all. He realised the woke folk enjoyed smashing up bits and pieces from yesteryear. They were like a bunch of school kids wrecking some past generation's toys and then wondering why they were not popular with that past generation.

From Primary school onwards, he understood that logic did not always dominate people's thinking. There was faith—something the system plugged into and manipulated. But where did it come from, and why?

A god such as Zeus hurling thunderbolts made sense when there was no other explanation for lightning. The seas could be rough, and so Poseidon was born.

Centuries later, King James the First of England and the Sixth of Scotland believed witches and warlocks were responsible for the wild weather that had attacked his ships. He wrote a book about witchcraft and how there was a need to stamp it out. This inevitably led to harming folk who had done no wrong but, in the eyes of superstitious men and women, were working magic against them. Thou shalt not suffer a witch to live was put into the King James Bible. It should have been thou shalt not suffer a poisoner to live, but the scribes, wanting to make the king happy and deciding that a witch would also be a poisoner, replaced poisoner with the word witch.

In medieval Europe, when people were dying from diseases, such as the Black Plague, there had to be a God responsible or at least willing to look the other way, allowing the Devil to have his fun. If there were only one God, all that could be done to possibly placate the Almighty and not be menaced by the Devil had to be done.

Great cathedrals were erected in the hope that God would be pleased. These structures took generations to complete, and it was no doubt hoped that God would be patient. Not all of it, though, was Christian. As far as Ross understood, gargoyles were positioned on such structures to scare away evil despite no mention of them in the Old or New Testament. They were pagan, and they were there.

No one cared what peasants thought in the Middle Ages, just as long as they did what they were told to do. If they had a secret belief system that didn't stop them from going to church or working in the fields, then that was all right, as long as the Church authorities didn't get wind of it. Occasionally, peasants rebelled and had to be reminded who ruled over them. Ross understood that there had been uprisings in France before the French Revolution. It succeeded mainly because the developing middle class joined forces with the peasantry.

At college, Ross's history lecturer once remarked that workers melting lead for lead-lined windows for these great cathedrals probably did see angels or demons. They were created in their minds by prolonged exposure to the fumes. No doubt, talk of angels or demons impacted the builders, indicating that God was pleased with their actions, while the Devil was not. Ross understood that, in modern times, workers dealing with lead fumes wore protective gas masks since too much exposure can not only damage the brain but also kill.

Ross realised that accounts of angels were found in Christianity, Judaism, and the Muslim faith. Did that mean they were real? There was another possibility. This was the flight that had long been a dream of humanity. Was that where angels came from? Ross wasn't sure. He liked the idea that they were God's messengers on Earth. Did people see them before they died? Could they make the transition between our world and the excellent beyond more accessible? Were they pleasant or terrifying to look at?

When just out of college, Ross had a friend dying of cancer. He was in his fifties and believed in angels. Because of this belief, the end was not as traumatic as it might have been. Had an angel helped his friend find a better form of existence? He hoped that was the case.

It wasn't until the invention of the microscope that people were able to get an understanding of bacteria. Before that discovery, there were very few answers to mysterious deaths. Bad smells were a clue. Diseased people didn't smell nice, just as meat that had gone off was unpleasant to the nose. Could good smells combat the bad and thus save lives? Ross understood that this was the reason for nosegays, the practice of bringing flowers to the sick, and the rising popularity of perfume in the Middle Ages.

Perfume, however, had been around longer than in medieval times. It is mentioned in the New Testament, but its use is probably even older than that. It was in the 17th Century that capturing good smells and bottling them became the science it is today, or so Ross learned from one of his lecturers. The rather unusual film Perfume was released in 2006. Was it possible to create a scent that all humans would be attracted to? Ross didn't think so, though he could imagine people trying to make such a perfume.

In college, Ross read about a pope who was advised to surround himself with fire to prevent becoming a plague victim. Hence, he had fires lit and maintained all around him by his servants. It worked. Others died, but the pope lived. The insects spreading the disease couldn't escape the flames to infect him.

Ross also read about the Flagellants. They were holy men who whipped each other in remembrance of how Jesus was once mistreated. In this way, in sympathy with Jesus, they hoped to obtain God's mercy for everyone. The pope of the day approved of them at first, but when they spoke out against the Church's accumulated wealth, they were excommunicated and then hunted down and eliminated.

In college, Ross experimented with marijuana. It acted like a mild sedative until one day, he got visions from it. Luckily, these visions occurred in his dorm room, and he was smart enough not to cry out. What he saw was smoke and something dancing in it. He couldn't make out anything else. He continued his experiment for extended periods, but the effect did not return. He did come across someone, years later, in the Rocks part of Sydney, who claimed marijuana had him seeing objects brighter than he had ever seen them before or ever since.

For Ross, fear of the black cat crossing one's path didn't make much sense until he discovered, through his college history lecturer, that those felines were supposed to be a witch's familiar, their link to the Devil.

Sometime later, he came across a New Zealand writer fond of black cats. Were they her familiars, and was witchcraft one reason she succeeded as a novelist? He didn't think so, but knew she would find such a conclusion amusing.

She lived in a hilly rather than mountainous part of New Zealand. He visited her old farm during a drought in New South Wales, Australia, and the central north island, New Zealand. Heavy rainfall occurred in New South Wales and New Zealand two years later. By then, COVID-19 was around, blocking further visits.

He returned to New Zealand in the summer three years later, when COVID-19 had died down. By this time, his New Zealand friend had a new cat companion she was fond of.

Some considered picking up a coin off the sidewalk bad luck. Was this a modern superstition? Ross knew of kids who put robust and fast-acting glue, such as Tarzan's Grip, on coins, making them difficult, if not impossible, to pick up off a footpath. He thought this was a mean trick, and it was not something he would ever do.

After his parents had passed away, Ross found himself thinking more and more about the possibility of what might exist beyond death. He missed them and wished he could have done more for them when they were alive. His mother would have liked to see him settled and married, but that was not the case in her lifetime. He wanted to believe in Heaven because that was the destination his parents deserved. Later, he wanted to believe in the just rewards, not just for himself, but also for his sister, his college friend Penelope, and his lady. Was this just wishful thinking? He hoped it was more than that.

If there is a Heaven, Ross figured ghosts must also be real. Throughout the world, in dozens of religions, there were ghost stories. Some dealt with shadowy humans, while others encountered animals that were no longer alive but still present. The fact that there was so much of this sort of thing tended to lend itself to the belief that it was for real.

In England, there were once wolves. They were hunted to extinction. By the 17th Century, they were thought to be gone forever, but tales persisted of ghost wolves roaming forest areas, menacing people at night.

Ross discovered, through his college studies, that in 19th-century English fiction, there were tales of monks as shades menacing the living because of what had happened to them and their monasteries during the reign of Henry VIII. With the Church of England taking over from Catholicism, the monasteries were gutted of what treasures they might hold, and the monks were poverty-stricken with no place to stay. It was particularly detrimental for those who attempted to block this change. The new church authority was far from gentle with those who resisted this takeover.

In New South Wales, Australia, there were haunted hotels near railroad stations and trees where men in the past had been hanged until dead. There were also bush stories about deceased Aborigines coming back to torment those who had wronged them in life.

One hotel caught his attention. It had been on the Cobb and Co. stage run before the railways came. A pregnant woman, in search of the man who had deserted her, stopped off there and was murdered. It was considered a robbery since her purse was stolen. Legend has it she wanders the corridors of this hotel at night, lantern in hand, in search of the villain who had ended her life and that of her child.

Ross's mother had been raised in the Church of England tradition, where angels tended to be young women with wings. From Henry VIII onward, with a gap created by Bloody Mary, who was Catholic, the

Church was governed by the leading monarch of England. For decades, going from the 20th to the 21st Century, Elizabeth II was head of this Church. Her son, Charles, who became King after her death, did not firmly believe in the Church. If he were not a firm believer, then how could he rule? Ross reasoned he would rule badly, and he was right. What he knew about Charles was that he had too much reverence for other religions to be a practical head of a Christian movement. There were signs of this in his Christmas speeches. Moreover, Charles wanted to distribute money to people whose ancestors may have been enslaved. This is even though over two hundred years ago, the British brought an end to slavery in the British Empire and fought against slavery elsewhere in the world.

"I don't understand religious politics," Ross once told Glenda over dinner, and she said she didn't understand them herself. They both understood the trouble religion could cause and that staying out of the firing line was best. Trouble in Ireland was only finally settled in the late 20th Century, and big problems remained in the Middle East.

American presidents have tried to be peacemakers in Middle Eastern affairs for generations, but generally, their efforts have been to little avail. How sincere were they in doing so? Ross imagined some of them just going through the motions because that's what the world wanted them to do. Who was entitled to what land and why? This was always a dispute, and Ross could see that it continued long after his lifetime.

He was aware of a time when Americans didn't want to be the problem solvers of the rest of the world. After the First World War, many Americans opposed joining the League of Nations, fearing continued entanglement in European conflicts. This was also why the United States entered the Second World War late. However, after the Second World War, a fear of a communist takeover led to a shift in American attitudes toward the rest of the world. Would it have been altered again if Red China had become more militant? Ross thought this might be the case.

Was woke the new Marxist spirit attacking the West, first in the universities and then on the internet, something to do with attempts to weaken Western-style democracy? Ross didn't know, but there were signs of democracy weakening.

Glenda believed in the spirit world, and, to some extent, near the end of their two good years together, so did Ross. The third and final not-so-great year together was the year of cancer for Ross. He could imagine in those years what it would be like to be a shade, wandering the earth because he needed revenge or lacked love.

He had come across a late medieval poem, probably also a song, about a young man who had died for the love of a young lady. He then took up haunting her. There was also a poem, probably a song, about a young woman who died from lack of love and became a discontented ghost.

Now, Glenda was with him, and Ross figured he had no desire for revenge against those who had supported the system. Since he had her love, he had no requirement to seek it elsewhere. Hence, he did not need to wander in such a way after death. He could then make the trip to the pearly gates.

Was there logic behind a belief in the pearly gates? Ross didn't think so, but he still hoped there was a God who cared for humanity. Glenda agreed with this assessment.

Was there Hell? Ross didn't know, nor did he care to find out. One Christian cult Ross read about had it that there were only Heaven and Hell. You are born into Hell, which is another name for the Earth, and if you are good, you ascend to Heaven after death—no third option. A crusade in France wiped out this cult. It was the cheapest of the Crusades since the Crusaders didn't have to leave Europe to see action.

CHAPTER THREE

Who Makes the Rules Anyway?

Unwritten rules of behaviour were still present in society as a system. They related to Australia's Judeo-Christian heritage and the notion that certain preachers regarded celibacy as good. But how do you fight the unwritten system? One answer was to be a bad guy and then later reform. In Christianity, if in no other religion, you could do wrong, say sorry, and be rewarded.

He didn't think this was the case regarding Islam, but he didn't know enough about it to comment accurately. Islam had only risen to importance in Australia when he was an adult, and it would have to do more with others making their way in society than with himself. It still scared the hell out of him. One thing he didn't want to be governed by was Sharia Law. Was Sharia Law on the cards for everyone living in Australia in the future? He shuddered at the thought.

Glenda Evens hadn't been responsible for the system, and he was glad of this. Perhaps she had been a victim of it. He couldn't see why those whom the system had mistreated had to be all men. He thought the system might be an equal opportunity destroyer of dreams and life.

She barely understood what it was all about, though she did agree with Ross that there was something about the society they had both grown up in that wasn't quite the way it should have been. She also decided it wasn't always easy for like-minded people to get together. Even the internet wasn't much help unless you were into a sport or another recognisable activity.

He had to wonder if alcoholism and the system were related, but he was never an alcoholic. The temptation had been there. If he had stayed at college longer, he might have become one, but that was not to be his fate. Glenda was happy with one glass of wine for the evening, and that was it. In his final years, Ross had a single beer in a pub, but it had to be a stinking hot day in the middle of summer.

No one Ross knew had made up the system's rules, but they were there. They were waved in his face at school and especially at Sunday school. They were on gravestones at cemeteries and were ingrained in most adults he met, even the ones who had gone against it and had gotten away with doing so. It was the getting away with stuff that intrigued Ross the most. He wanted to do it earlier in life, but didn't know how. He discovered it required a partner, someone else willing to do it with him. That much he came to understand. If he were Clyde, he needed a Bonnie. And they had to make their getaway!

In the 1960s, according to a newspaper article he read, the Salvation Army was unhappy with the James Bond movies due to Bond's uncomplicated sex life. As a kid, Ross knew these films were based on fantasy, not reality. Bond, as the kind of spy he was made out to be, couldn't exist. He stood out too much and, in standing out, couldn't infiltrate. The notion of a license to kill, Ian Fleming, the author of the original novels, claimed, was his tongue-in-cheek nonsense that readers enjoyed. He knew real spies from World War II and understood that his Bond had more fiction than fact about it.

Could the Bond films contribute to an increase in teenage pregnancies? Ross didn't think so since no one could be Bond in real life or think they could be like Bond. Years later, Ross understood that these films could not have had that much influence in his world except as a form of escape from it, either in the cinema or the drive-in. The notion that it would take a British spy to prevent the Russians and Americans from declaring war on each other and thus blowing up the world was ludicrous, though somewhat charming.

Ross realised in his teens that women had a different way of looking at sex. As a male, he saw it as a barrier to overcome in a relationship. He figured everything else would fall into place once it had been achieved. Otherwise, they would remain just friends for whatever that was worth.

According to the system, sex was something to be hidden away and forgotten until the time came when this was no longer the case. The trick was to discover when it was appropriate to discuss and participate in it. The system liked people to be afraid. The only winners were those brave enough to risk what must be risked.

Women get pregnant, and children are born. This is not complicated, but it is made more so by self-righteous preachers out to save the planet from too many offspring arriving too quickly for society to cope with. As for responsibility, how can anyone be responsible when it is not in their hands? Responsibility requires the person to have the choice of doing good or ill. Ross felt he had never been given responsibility for what he felt in life he should be personally responsible for as a thinking human being.

Would the world be better if fewer children lived in it? This view was widely held in Australia in the 1960s and 1970s. An episode of the American television show Star Trek pointed to the possibility of a planet that is too overcrowded with humanoids. Was this meant as a warning to humanity in general? Ross thought so.

By 2023, smaller family units in Australia meant that retirement on a pension shifted from age 65 to 67 and later to 70. This was also an argument in favour of further immigration. Was this further immigration the system's plan all along? Cut down on the number of children born in Australia so that importing people to fill so-called gaps makes sense? Ross thought this was a possibility.

From the mid-1970s onward, many people fled conflict zones to countries such as the United States, Canada, the United Kingdom, and Australia. People out to break the backs of Western-style countries went with the genuine refugees. This pattern would continue for decades as new wars emerged.

Vietnamese Catholics needed to get away from a communist state that saw them as the enemy. Later, it would be Afghans fleeing the Taliban because they didn't want to live under the thumb of brutal Muslim fanatics. They were still Muslims, but a gentler kind that enjoyed good food, dance, non-religious music, and the more traditional aspects of their faith.

Then there were the cheats claiming to be refugees but skipping past countries where they could settle for places where they wanted to live. Ross knew this was what had happened in the early 21ˢᵗ Century in the UK with people from Africa. They could stay in France, but wanted to go to England instead.

The system was in place to be fought against and defied, and those who had done so were either punished or rewarded. He imagined sneaking up on it from behind, this system thing, wrestling it to the ground and stabbing it through the heart. This, of course, could never be because it was not a person. It wasn't made up of anything solid one could ever lay hands upon. He could just as well have had some notion of doing in a cloud because it rained on him or punching his shadow because he didn't like its looks.

At age twenty-one, Ross had a full-time job but no girlfriend. He got a digital watch for his birthday and a new suit. The suit was purple and was bought at a store in Bankstown that was going out of business. The salesman didn't take him to the Men's section for suits but to the junior section. He should have known getting a suit there was a bad idea. The truth was that none of the so-called adult suits would fit him. Maybe in another store, they would. The purple monstrosity he picked out with his mother. If he had been there, his dad would have talked him out of it. But what did Ross know about suits? Nothing. So, he was easy prey, and so was his mother.

Over the years, Ross had acquired several suits but always felt much more comfortable in jeans and T-shirts in summer and checkered, long-sleeved shirts and jeans in winter. It was no-fuss wear, unlikely to cost much, and unlikely to harm him. From the purple suit onwards, he thought of suits as treacherous.

At age twenty-one plus, Ross walked into a pub in Sydney and asked for a beer. The bastard behind the counter wanted to see ID. Since Ross didn't have any ID, he didn't get a drink. He didn't particularly enjoy beer. It was a test of his coming of age, being over twenty-one, and failing. He wasn't tall, and he was skinny. The bastard looked after his livelihood, but Ross couldn't see it that way. What was the point of being over twenty-one, an adult with a job, if no one would treat you that way? And how should young women see him as a man under these circumstances?

When he was twenty-five, Ross went to a league club with his family. There was a sectioned-off area for dining where they could serve alcohol. His sister, Kate, two years younger than he, breezed past the bouncers without a problem, but they stopped him. "Are you over twenty-one?" asked one of them. "Yes," said Ross in a matter-of-fact voice. He tried to move forward, but that was not allowed. "Do you have ID?" He was asked. "No," was his reply. "Can anyone vouch for him?" asked the other bouncer. The bouncer was kind and generous, but Ross didn't see it that way. The safari suit he was wearing didn't help much since most guys his age, including himself, look lousy in such attire. Ross got red in the face as his father did the vouching. He was let in, but Ross would take a long time to forgive the league club and contact sports for their treatment. Again, it was only people protecting what they felt needed protecting. But how would he ever get on if this kept happening to him?

After Ross got a driver's license, he thought his fortunes would change. This was not long after the incident at the league club. He decided to test this license by seeing an R-rated horror movie at a cinema. It was *The Demons; he* thought it would have amusing special effects. The ticket woman took the fun away by overly scrutinising his driver's license as if it were probably a fake. Reluctantly, she took his money and gave him his ticket. Because of her, he did not enjoy the movie as much as he would have.

By the time Ross entered college in his thirties, he could be recognised as over twenty-one, but what use was that? He had had a decade wandering about in the system's wilderness, failing to learn to make connections because he wasn't given much of any chance to do so. He should have tried harder. He should have known more about women and relationships in his thirties, but he knew virtually nothing and was pretending he knew something, anything, and it wasn't working. Was growing up this bloody difficult for others? In his thirties, there were women prepared to write him off entirely, and he had no idea what to do about it.

Rule number one in winning against the system was to get your act together before you are in your thirties, or you may never get anywhere with the opposite sex. You may get heaps of sympathy you don't need, leading to ruination.

Ross understood that religion played a role in creating and maintaining the system. Rule number two in fighting the system was to never talk about religion or do anything with it unless there was something in it for you. Ross's dad gave him this rule, and he was right to follow it.

According to his college studies, back during the First World War, there were Catholic priests in positions of power speaking out against the killing and opposed to conscription. Some took an Irish view in that many Irish Australians had ancestors shipped to Australia in chains and so felt no loyalty to England and, thus, to England's struggle against Germany.

When the Vietnam War rolled around, the Catholic Church rallied around a Vietnamese thug and did not, to Ross's knowledge, attack the notion of conscription for 1970s youth. By the end of the Vietnam War, there was a sense among Australians that not only had the Catholic leaders failed the people, but that this was a general Christian failure.

Ross discovered that making love, not war, had nothing to do with discos. Despite looking younger than he was, he was permitted to enter such places. There was freedom here, but only in the consumption of alcohol.

Ross was too young to be conscripted at the time of the Vietnam War. He was old enough to be affected by it. He had a cousin who was sent to the war and came back with wounds of both body and mind. He told Ross that there were ways to win the war. There were places troops could have been sent, but were not allowed to go. The object, then, for at least the Americans, wasn't a total win but a compromise like in Korea. There was a fear that a significant victory would draw the Chinese army into the conflict, and the USA was unprepared to face those odds. When a compromise was no longer possible, the war ended with the enemy as the victor.

New religions gained a foothold in Sydney due to a distrust of Christianity. There were the Orange People, who were around in the 1970s and 1980s. Scientology had existed since the 1950s but gained significant popularity in the 1970s. The young seemed to seek something not found in the age-old Christian beliefs.

Ross found Robert M. Pirsig's novel Zen and the Art of Motorcycle Maintenance a revelation. He also enjoyed Richard Bach's Jonathan Livingston Seagull. He investigated Buddhism but found it was not for him. The philosophy behind it was fine, but the structure reminded him too much of Christianity.

He didn't think Judaism was for him, but thought it was okay for others.

Ross would never forget his introduction to Methodist beliefs. It was every Sunday for a year, weighing down on him. He felt it was enough to have school five days a week. Sitting on a pew and listening to a sad preacher rattle on about a guy who was crucified over two thousand years ago, and what we owed him was too much. Moreover, the boys sat to the left and the girls to the right. This was serious business. It has nothing to do with frivolity or kids getting to know other kids. It was all such dull, miserable stuff, yet his dad thought it would benefit him.

Pupils stopped attending that Sunday school class. When Ross got pneumonia, it was his way out. He was in a Primary classroom during the working week when he came to be underwater with books and papers floating about. He felt dizzy and asked to be excused to go home to sort his head out. His mother got the doctor over, and Ross spent weeks in bed trying not to throw up. He was provided with comic books and an Astro Boy toy. When it was over, his dad gave him an ice cream cone, which he thoroughly enjoyed. His dad also asked him if he wanted to return to that Sunday school, and he said No way.

What he remembered most about those Sunday school lessons was forgiveness. He later came to think of it as the most insidious part of Christianity. You sin; you are forgiven. Sounds pretty good. In practice, it appeared to benefit others rather than himself. When it came to lust, he wanted to sin like crazy, be forgiven, and then sin like mad even more, but that wasn't to be.

Ross, in his late teens, would have loved to have run around with lots of girls his age and have sex with them. He figured that with the pill and condoms, that would be fine. Of course, that Methodist preacher had been against that sort of thing on the off chance some young woman might still get pregnant. This preacher was married with kids. Did he arrive at that station in life the right or wrong way? Ross never knew.

Ross wondered why his brother, Ian, never had to attend that Sunday school. He also wondered why his sister, Kate, hadn't been roped in. Kate got religion not long after he had finished with that Methodist preacher. How did that happen? He had no answers. It may have had something to do with the boy she was going out with and would eventually marry.

In his travels, Ross heard about a pregnant woman and her companion entering a small church to pray and was asked by the priest not to return. It was a case of no ring on her finger. This upset some of his parishioners. *Why was it so?* Ross wondered. *And where was the forgiveness bit?*

Ross had all sorts of answers in his head as to why this had come about. Maybe some of these stodgy men and women had married, which had all gone wrong, but they were stuck with it. Others may have never married or had much to do with sex, and they regretted it to the point that they hated anyone who had ever taken a chance on someone else.

The pregnant woman who had entered the church got married to her companion, so everything, according to Christian beliefs, turned out as it should. Neither of them returned to that church, so Ross was informed.

When he found out his brother, Ian, had got a young woman pregnant, Ross felt numb. He had been warned so often not to get a young woman in such a way, but here it had happened, with his brother at fault, if there was a fault. His parents were initially shocked but made the best of it, helping the couple where possible. Maybe they had more of the Christian spirit than those parishioners and that priest at that church. They had more of that going for them than Ross had at the time. Forgiveness and getting on with life did seem like the best way to go, but what could Ross make out of that?

What life was he supposed to get on with? It seemed to Ross that certain people had the golden ticket they didn't deserve, and he had to do the best he could with whatever native intelligence he had. It just wasn't fair.

This unfairness was to drag him down. What he should have realised was how it all tended to balance out. Shallow hangers-on might forever pester a good-looking man or woman until they were no longer so good-looking. Someone always getting into trouble might end up dead sooner rather than later, even if they did all right sooner. Some guys married young but couldn't make a go of it, and then some young women found themselves deserted when they needed help the most.

Was fairness ever a real thing, anyway? He knew the government had long ago created a minimum wage system for all Australian workers. You couldn't hire anyone and pay them below this wage. Then, work for the dole came along, and there was a way to pay someone below minimum wage and get away with it.

There were high school graduates with slim prospects, and by the 1990s, entering the trades had become significantly more challenging. He once met a young chap who had just landed a railway job. After years on the dole, he was ecstatic about finally having a solid future. He could marry his girlfriend and someday own his own home.

People in their 50s and 60s were unlikely to secure further employment and were not encouraged to improve themselves. Job agencies could have been more helpful. They were more interested in obtaining government funding than getting people to work.

Maybe reincarnation came into play in all of this. Could his brother and others have gotten hints on how best to act from previous lives? If Ross had lived before, he suspected it was as a monk, so he had no prior knowledge about the opposite sex that he could conjure up in his mind from another, earlier existence. If he died and came back in another body, would there be anything he could present his new self with that was worth anything? He considered it a sad no until he met Glenda, his lady love.

What would two years of the good times do to help him if he ever returned to another body? Very little, he thought, but it might be a good start. He could do better next time. He even contemplated being a bastard with a shorter life span but plenty of sex. But would that ever really be him? He didn't think so. There was something in his nature that would always rebel against the possibility of his taking up bastardry. Was it a case of cowardice on his part? No. That wasn't it. He just needed to see a way ahead, which wasn't always possible.

He once read somewhere that Jack the Ripper got away with all he did because he didn't overthink. He was an opportunist who took advantage of the opportunity to kill without being caught. Ross didn't want to kill anyone, but the notion of being an opportunist in the ways of love did make sense.

Ross saw himself as the overthinker who gets undone every time. But how do you change? How do you stop overthinking? Despite dipping into Zen in his twenties, it took Ross's old age to get there. He had to forget his brother's success and forgive himself for his failures.

CHAPTER FOUR

You Don't Hit Girls

Violence was something Ross Martin avoided. He couldn't see why he should get into a fight. Even so, he didn't care to be ruled over by anyone. He didn't want to be some wimp afraid to speak out about an injustice. In life, there were battles he had to fight without resorting to the use of his fists. He fought them and, at times, lost and, at other times, won.

Ross Martin had entered a peaceful life in his old age with the woman he loved. It wasn't always so. He remembered the first time he had ever contemplated revenge on a member of the opposite sex. It did not go well for him. It was at the beginning of his dealings with what he would later refer to as the system.

He was three and playing in a sandbox in his backyard when Jem, a neighbour's kid, wanted to take his spade away from him. She had one of her own but desired his instead. He refused to give it to her, so she bit him on the arm, sinking her teeth in. Outraged, he sprang up and howled, his little fist balling up. She screamed and ran away, and he followed her, determined to punish her for what she had done.

He felt he had every right to hit her. It was justice. Seeing a terrified Jem being chased by an angry Ross, Jem's mother chose her daughter's side. She turned the hose on him. His mouth and nose filled with water.

He found it hard to breathe. He was thus driven away. He told his story to his mother, showing her the bite mark as proof of Jem's wrongdoing. His mother told him You mustn't hit girls. Then, she went to Jem's mother and spoke about how she did not appreciate what had been done to her son.

This event stuck with Ross. He and Jem grew up on the same street but were never friends. She was always snotty toward him, and he preferred anyone else's company.

Her father made more money than his father, which was at the heart of her snottiness. He was glad when she moved away. Later, he was to learn she had married, had some kids, had a shop, and had been in a car accident. She was severely hurt. There, he lost contact completely. He never found out if she recovered in a hospital or not. He suspected she had done so, but it no longer mattered. She had not been his problem for too long, and it was best to leave it that way.

Ross's last memory of Jem was when he met her halfway up the road toward the local train station. He was fifteen at the time. She was with a group of kids his age. The first thing she did when she saw him was put him down. He would have liked to have gotten to know those other kids, but he knew that wouldn't happen because they were Jem's friends. He wanted to punch her then and there, but it wasn't the thing to do. You don't hit girls had sunk in. He would have liked to have made Jem an exception to that rule, but knew his mother, father, and sister wouldn't like it if he did.

Jem was a bully, but also popular. No one cared to cross her. He was thankful that he didn't attend the same high school as her. It was bad enough that she was at his kindergarten and then his primary school. Thank goodness she was in none of his classrooms. Not a single teacher seemed to understand she was no good. She was great at hiding her evil nature, especially when it might get her into trouble. She was big for her age with straggly brown hair and blue eyes.

Ross thought kindergarten would be an excellent place to make friends and learn about life. He hadn't counted on a medieval superstition getting in his way and causing him harm.

His teacher had lengthy brown hair and a long nose that dripped constantly, requiring a hanky to be handy, which was always in her sleeve. That's all he remembered of her, apart from the metal ruler. It was a shiny instrument made of stainless steel, something he would never forget in over fifty years of living.

Every time he tried to write with his left hand, that ruler would come down on his knuckles. He didn't recall crying. He did remember putting his hand under the tap at recess to let cold water take away some of the throbbing hurt. He tried to hide using his left hand when he wrote, but he'd always be found out. Then it was Whack! Whack! Whack! With the ruler to teach him a lesson. "You write with your right hand in my classroom!" the teacher said imperiously.

Ross came home one day with noticeable bruising and swelling on his left hand. His mother asked him if he had been in a fight. He said no and told her how his teacher got him to write with his right hand. The look of astonishment on his mother's face was something to behold. "Teachers are not supposed to do that," she told him. "Really?" he came out with. "Really," replied his mother. "So, no hitting should go both ways," he said. "I'll talk with this teacher," his mother told him. "Then I will discuss with whoever is in charge of that school."

The next day, his mother confronted the teacher and the kindergarten's head. Ross didn't remember what she said, but he was moved to another classroom and never saw the teacher with the dripping nose again. Thanks to that terrible teacher, though, he had to repeat a year. This, he thought, was entirely unfair.

Many years later, Ross was to read how some people took someone being left-handed as a sign of the Devil, of evil. Maybe that was what the teacher with the steel ruler was trying to do. Beat the Devil out of him. Was the Devil really in him? He had dark thoughts, but came to realise everyone had those anyway. Did he ever want to turn that steel ruler on the teacher? He didn't think so, but in old age, he couldn't remember everything to do with his childhood. In any event, the beatings didn't work. He remained a lefty for the rest of his life.

Ross's mother looked for famous lefties and came upon Errol Flynn, the Australian actor. Later, while viewing the Olympics in America, Ross found an Italian woman who was left-handed and a champion with a sword. He took up fencing at college and thoroughly enjoyed the experience. He also learned that Billy the Kid was once known as the "Left-Handed Gun." He later discovered that Billy's being left-handed may have had more to do with early photography than true left-handedness.

In primary, Ross came across other girls just as stuck-up as Jem. He also came upon one interested in whatever he was engrossed in. Her name was Linda, and she had a round face, short brown hair and a button nose. It was lunchtime, and he was at the back of the school, where there was lots of grass. There was a praying mantis he was going to catch. He contemplated this action a little too long. He was bent over in his study of the creature when Linda gently pushed him. He toppled over, and the praying mantis was gone.

"What are you doing?" she asked. Ross got to his feet and said, "There was a praying mantis." Linda thought about this and replied, "There was?" Ross sighed and said, "It's gone now!" Linda smiled and replied, "Too bad!" Years later, Ross discovered, through a friend, that Linda liked him and wanted to get to know him better.

There were two girls in his classroom, Tina and Trixie. They were twins and did everything they could to be individuals. Tina always had her black hair in ponytails, while Trixie always had her hair free, long, and wild. They had long faces and small mouths. There was no mistaking which had a conservative nature and which was rowdy. Ross liked both but preferred Tina's company.

The yo-yo had come back in fashion, sponsored by Coca-Cola, and Tina was the mistress of 'around the world' and 'walking the dog'. Ross found watching her play with a yo-yo fascinating. Girls were not supposed to be good at yo-yos, but she was excellent. She also skipped rope like a champion.

Everyone played marbles. No one was left out. There was no rule against girls being good at it, and some girls played well. Still, marbles were a game typically played in primary school rather than high school. When he left primary school, all interest in marbles ceased. It was not a game to be played in high school, since no one there was interested in playing.

He thought high school would be a place for academic achievement. He was wrong. Being lousy at Maths meant he was crippled intellectually, and the teachers were going to put him in classes where he was expected to learn zilch. He got a break with science for one year, but that was it. There was no chance of learning to read music, and no way was anyone going to teach him a foreign language. He was good at English, but that didn't count for some reason.

He imagined what it would be like to learn either French or German and then travel around Europe. He wanted to see great art and architecture, not just in books. In the end, even after leaving formal schooling, he never did learn a second language, not even through night school. He also never grasped music the way he wanted to. It is best to learn while the mind is still fresh to new possibilities, he concluded in his old age.

Europe was forever out of Ross's reach. It wouldn't have been when he was earning a decent living. At that stage in his life, though, he was sharing a house with a woman who wouldn't pay her bills on time. He would cover for her, and she would repay him. Then, more bills would come, and the cycle would start again. The result was that he never could get his finances together for trips. When he stopped covering for her, the bills were not paid on time, which was not good. Ultimately, he was glad to bow out of her life, but by then, he could see retrenchment looming and the end of a job he had had for ten years.

Ross should have gone to the high school dances, but couldn't see himself doing so after the tough times he had during the day. The night was for him and the television set. It wasn't a good decision and one he would later regret. There was a real world he should have been part of, which he neglected, thinking he would catch up with it later when he had more to offer. That later never came.

There were meatheads in his English and History classes. He was the brain-dead one in the classes he hated, such as Maths. There was a rumour going around that the teacher who was teaching Maths to his class drank during school hours and was tottering on becoming an alcoholic.

It was too late for Ross to discover that there was a theatre production at his high school. Because he needed to improve in Math and was not in the best English classes, he never learned what was on and whether he could take on one of the roles in the production.

A vocational guidance expert who talked to Ross before he left high school thought he might make a great landscape gardener. He rejected the notion. It felt like a put-down, even though he knew little about landscape gardening. He knew it had nothing to do with History or English. It might have been good for him, but he couldn't see it that way. He had never considered taking care of plants as a career path.

The other option was for him to work in a factory as a production line worker. This meant getting better at Metalwork, which he took as an even heavier, more blatant attack on who he was and wanted to be.

Ross spent six months sitting on his hands in the playground because there was no metalwork teacher. He would never forget or forgive this.

One day, a supervising teacher had Ross and the others in this so-called Metalwork class pick up loose rubbish in the playground. Ross hated this form of discrimination. The teacher blamed them for the litter being there in the first place because most of them were poor at Maths.

"You drop them at recess; you pick them up now," this teacher said imperiously. Ross complied. Then, for two weeks afterwards, he became a litterbug. The paper bag that his sandwiches from home came in missed the bin. Having been accused of a crime he had never committed, he felt it only fitting to commit that misdeed for a while. That supervising teacher made him feel like the lowest of the low, and he noticed the other students with him didn't like it either, but no one protested. Maybe some of them were guilty. He didn't know, nor did he ask.

Ross chose Metalwork over Woodwork because of a lousy Woodwork teacher who spent six months teaching him how to plane perfect wood blocks into matchsticks. "Put some muscle into it!" cried this teacher. Ross did so, and it was apparent that the muscles on one arm were more potent than the muscles on the other, making the plane move at an angle rather than straight. He discovered this when his father introduced him to someone better at Woodworking and showed him how to plane smoothly and effectively with much less effort and greater skill.

Once a Metalwork teacher was available, the class got stuck into various projects. Ross never learned who had taught some of these others he was with, those six months of nothing but warming a bench in the playground or picking up rubbish, but it was apparent most of the class now knew a lot more than he did about the subject. He felt cheated, and it showed. He was resentful of the teacher and the students. He might have given the teacher more of a go, but that wasn't in him. He didn't reflect on how difficult it must have been to inherit a class with zero action at its first introduction to his subject. Years later, he realised that the teacher might have been of more help to him if he had only asked.

There was also a kind of mad hatred that came with being the class fool. At one time, he came close to jabbing a student with a screwdriver for a remark that had been made. The teacher wanted him to stay back after school, but he refused. He began skipping class. He was a bad boy, but realised he was the wrong kind. It's not the type of bad behaviour girls go for.

There was a place close to his high school where kids from his school went to smoke, drink and take drugs. He encountered it only once and was happy to be sworn to secrecy and never return. They thought he might report them, but that wasn't what he was about. He had no reason to mess with their lives. He wondered how those kids got to smoke, drink, and take drugs, but never asked. He didn't care to smoke but figured he couldn't afford to drink or play around with drugs.

When he was placed in Technical Drawing, his hatred for Maths ensured he would never be good at it.

What he learned in Technical Drawing aided him in his discovery and understanding of late medieval paintings and architecture. Techniques developed then gave a small space the illusion of being larger using perspective and the right colours. It often came down to where the painter had directed the eyes of anyone looking at his work and what was there for them to see.

Years later, he was to discover that the factories the school was driving male students into were not to last. It was much cheaper to make stuff overseas, and so, within a decade, those factories were but a memory.

Ross's sister, Kate, would have liked to study woodwork, but that was not for girls. It was a school policy. Decades later, she took it up and excelled at it, but this did not compensate for her hurt from being excluded from such a study.

Ross would have liked to have learned how to type because he wanted to be a writer, but typing was considered a feminine skill at that school. It would have been a good idea if every high school student had studied typing because of the growing popularity of computers in offices and other areas of employment. Even being in a warehouse meant you had to know something about computers and be able to work a keyboard.

Ross imagined someday being a famous novelist and having a secretary to do his typing. That never happened. In old age, though, he got Glenda to edit his short stories before they were sent to the world. She said she was happy to do this for him.

Glenda collected stamps and had a good collection from around the world. Ross thought the ones from Australia and New Zealand were a cut above the rest. He especially liked the ones featuring native birds and lizards. He felt the American and British stamps were generally plain-looking.

When he asked her why she collected them, she said, "They're art—an inexpensive form anyone can have to keep."

Ross remembered Jackie, a high school girl who also collected stamps. He remembered giving her one or two in the playground. She thanked him, smiled, and ran off. How did he know she collected? He overheard her say so to a girl in class.

Looking back, Ross knew he could have done more with Jackie in high school. She was a cute brunette in his English class with hazel eyes. She occasionally smiled at him. He should have talked to her more and maybe gone out with her. Unfortunately, Math, Woodwork, Metalwork, and Technical Drawing had gotten him down to where he felt like a shadow rather than a person.

He thought getting out and finding a good job would set him up well to meet young women around his age and then move on with his life. He was wrong.

Leaving high school behind, Ross didn't want to hit anyone, but he would have liked to have kissed a young woman. Was that so wrong? It seemed to be a natural enough want. It was also being ever so personal with someone else. He was trepidatious about that. He figured it would be ever so easy to step out of line. He wasn't even sure where the line was drawn or why.

While working in a government office, his thoughts sometimes concerned his brother, Ian, and how he had boldly entered fatherhood and marriage. Could he do the same? He didn't think so. Perhaps this was because he couldn't imagine himself doing so.

Ross wasn't much of a gambler, and as time went by and he kept his office job, this became even less so. He might bet on the Melbourne Cup, but that was it. The Melbourne Cup was the horse race that most people in Australia had a flutter on. One year, he even won. He didn't have enough money on it, however, to make himself an instant millionaire.

While working in a factory in Riverwood, Ross encountered a worker who consistently bet $200 on the Melbourne Cup. The worker told Ross he figured a big win one year would set him up for life. He didn't bet during the rest of the year, just on the Melbourne Cup. As far as Ross knew, that fellow never did get that big win.

How would his brother have gone with a desk job? He didn't know, nor was he ever able to find out. Being married and happily so, he might have done all right. If anyone wanted to hassle him for being too taken with any of the women, he could flash his wedding ring and say I am uninterested. Chances are, it would be the truth. But what if his brother hadn't been married at all? In that case, it would probably have been for the best that most of his brother's jobs had been blue-collar and, thus, for a bloke, reasonably safe.

In the end, Ross had to admit that comparing himself to Ian, his brother, was dumb. They could never have lived similar lives because they had different temperaments and body shapes. Both could buy into victimhood from various angles, and both, he knew, were better off not doing so.

Ian's wife would never be Ross's friend, which was a pity and, in part, his fault. He had tried at times to get along with her, but it simply wasn't to be. Sometimes, you have to cut your losses and move on.

In old age, around the breakfast table, Ross didn't think it was wicked to kiss someone you liked, but it was always her, Glenda, his lady love, that did the kissing, not him. He remained gun-shy about initiating that sort of thing.

CHAPTER FIVE

Playing Soldier

At an early age, Ross Martin understood that soldiers could die in battle. It was apparent even to a five-year-old living in Australia. The system had it that death in combat was glorious. He realised it wasn't magnificent at all except for the knowing sacrifice. There was the notion of giving one's life so that the society to which they belonged might continue to exist. This was fine if there could be, through such sacrifice, an end to war. This hope had so far been unfulfilled.

The last post played on a trumpet is eerie, unsettling, and sad. The first time Ross heard it, it nearly brought him to tears. It reminded him of how vulnerable every soldier had been in his country's history.

Ross Martin realised, growing up, that those who thought the First World War would be the end of war were naïve. Perhaps they only believed there would never be another world war. In this, they were proven wrong. There was the League of Nations, created to prevent war, but it turned out to be toothless, and so, in the end, it couldn't stop the Second World War from happening. Was the United Nations much better? He didn't think so. What had stopped the more significant nations from going to war directly with one another in the 20th Century was the threat of a nuclear holocaust.

But what happens when you have religious nutters happy to murder themselves and their families just so long as their enemies also die? Thus, destruction of everything, thanks to a maniacal death cult with nuclear weapons, remains possible to this day.

When he was very young in kindergarten, Ross watched these kids go up this slope in the playground with sticks to face other kids who also had sticks atop the hill. The kids at the top were taking on the roles of German soldiers. The kids walking bravely up the slope were pretending to be Americans. The sticks were supposed to be rifles, and some pretend Americans got shot while walking up the hill. Some kids imagined having hand grenades called pineapples. They launched them at the make-believe Germans after pretending to pull out the pin with their teeth. They then made explosion noises, and the pretend Germans fell on cue.

One day, Ross asked to join in and was initially made a German, then graduated to become one of the tough Americans. He recalled getting shot and blown up a lot, but all in good fun. They acted like they were in *Combat*, an American television series. It dealt with the American push into France during World War II, beginning on June 6, 1944, with the D-Day landings. Strangely enough, this TV series lasted longer than the year it covered during the war.

Many years later, Ross saw *Combat* on DVD and wasn't disappointed. The acting was good, but the background and special effects were sensational. Most of the show's runs were in black and white. It moved to colour but wasn't as action-packed, and the background scenery wasn't quite as impressive. Even so, Ross could see why he and others were taken with the show when he was a kid.

Spyforce, an Australian show about World War II produced in the 1970s, didn't have quite the same appeal to Ross as *Combat*. It was in colour but always looked cheap and poorly put together, as if it lacked a budget. The main fun he got out of the show was when he discovered that one of the actors, called upon to play a Japanese soldier, was a Chinese Australian who ran a local toy shop. He remembered buying a chattering, mobile skull from him, a wind-up toy that fitted into one's hand. He and other kids would show up at his shop and ask him to put on the mean Japanese face he had on television, which he was happy to do for them. They and Ross knew it was just acting since, in real life, he was a nice guy.

Sometime after the show *Combat,* the *Shintaro* craze started. Scanlens sold packets containing cards with still photos from the show, accompanied by their brand of chewing gum. Kids eagerly snapped up these cards. Ross had a collection of them. He was also into the show. He found the adventures of *Shintaro the Samurai* much more entertaining than that preacher he had to listen to on a Sunday. After he got home from church, he happily parked himself in front of the TV set to enjoy Japanese swordplay mixed with ninja magic. It didn't bother him then that the Japanese were the villains in *Spyforce* and *McHale's Navy,* whereas in Shintaro, some were the heroes.

Ross would have loved to see *Shintaro* live, but his parents couldn't afford the tickets to the show. It was staged in Sydney.

Soon after Ross's bout with pneumonia, *Gigantor* and *Astro Boy started appearing on television; they were animated Japanese shows in black and white with English voices, initially produced* by Americans for an American audience. Gigantor was a giant robot operated by a young boy. Astroboy was a robot that looked like a boy but could fly and fight bad guys and robots acting up. There was plenty of action and heart in such shows as well. It got Ross into reading more science fiction, such as Isaac Asimov's and Ray Bradbury's stories.

Ross recalled how the 1960s Astro Boy was much better than later versions. What was shown on Australian television and in colour in the 1980s had a much slower pace than the original and thus less appeal.

Because of *Shintaro*, *Gigantor*, and *Astroboy*, Ross was not prepared to work in an office with a Japanese woman who detested the Chinese and thought of white Australians as second-class English. He needed to adjust to her. At this time, the system had its claws deep into him, and he was looking for comfort in getting on with whatever work was given.

Hearing her spout racist remarks about the Chinese, the Islanders, plus the Australians did not help. It was a clash of cultures, and the politically correct had it that anyone, not Anglo-Saxon Australian, should win in such a clash. A woman whose grasp on reality was tainted with past Japanese imperialism was someone Ross didn't want to be lumbered with. He endured her company until he could leave that office with some money behind him.

Decades later, his sister, Kate, came to work for a Japanese tyre company. Half the people she worked with and for were Japanese. She told Ross she got along fine with them. They had quirks, such as a fascination with playing golf without spending a fortune. Also, where they lived in Sydney, they had a lawn to mow and a large garden to tend. These things could not be readily enjoyed in Japan unless you were wealthy.

Ross thought maybe the Japanese woman he had been saddled with was a one-off. The Japanese Kate worked with were no doubt generations removed from all that imperialist stuff, and so were the new Japanese who did their best to get along with everyone.

As for children and their toys, Ross recalled the fuss made by some parent groups in the 1980s over the *Mutant Ninja Turtles* craze. Was it really okay for kids to pretend to be these cartoon characters and battle one another with toy swords? One interviewer recalled kids of his generation dressed up as cowboys with cap guns. Then, they mentioned kids playing American soldiers and, finally, Samurai or ninjas. "It's all part of growing up," the interviewer concluded, "and nothing to get strung out about."

Ross's father impressed upon him, as best he could, the real horrors of war and how it was great not to go into battle. This view was enforced by the American television show *MASH* and later by the Australian movie *Gallipoli* (1981), the mini-series ANZACS (1985), and still later by *ANZAC Girls* (2014). Ross understood that mateship, which should last forever, was forged during the First World War and, many years later, became a thorn in the side of both political correctness and the subsequent woke movement.

At college, there were students against ANZAC Day and the marching of old soldiers on television. Ross understood that many of them had never had family members in uniform or had listened to World War I veterans talk of the awfulness of armed combat. As far as Ross was concerned, not one single veteran on television was in praise of war. After having lived through terrible battles, they were all in favour of peace and an end to war.

They linked up with old comrades on ANZAC Day and talked about mates who never came home. Two-Up was legal on that one day a year and was played everywhere. He remembered seeing it played at Revesby and, on another occasion, at Bathurst. There was a blanket, a stick, and two coins to be tossed. At Revesby, he had been too young to play. At Bathurst, he didn't have much money and didn't want to gamble away what he had.

The tradition continued, and veterans from the Second World War, the Korean War, and the Vietnam War followed the same pattern as those of the First World War. There was controversy over whether sons and daughters should be allowed to march, wearing their medals, in the place of veterans unable to do so. Eventually, it was decided that this was all right as World War One soldiers had thinned out to none, and this would someday happen to the World War Two veterans.

There was also a minute of silence on the eleventh hour, the eleventh day, and the eleventh month. This was the remembered armistice that brought World War One to a close, but it went further than that, encompassing all such endings. It was a time to recall those who didn't come back. It was also for prayer, the most common being ending all future wars.

In the 1990s, Ross learned that a high school principal stopped the minute of silence at her school because she thought Turkish migrants new to her area would be offended by it. They were offended, all right, but by her stopping it, since in their culture, they respected that moment of silence. Also, they were angered at being made her scapegoats in the matter. They wanted to get along with their fellow Australians.

In the early 21st century, people in South Australia were keen on abolishing ANZAC Day and Christmas. He took them to be lunatic Woke and hoped they wouldn't ever get away with it.

"The best warriors only fight when it is necessary to do so," his dad once told Ross.

His grandfather, who came close to being killed in France during the First World War, had nothing to say on the subject. He just waved away any discussion before him on the matter of war. The shrapnel he carried did his talking for him.

Ross's grandfather was a tall, lanky man even in old age. He had been born in a London slum. As a boy, his grandfather dipped fat from the previous night's meal on bread for breakfast since jam was too expensive. From an early age, his grandfather learned that food was too precious and not to be wasted. This attitude undoubtedly helped him and his family through shortages during the Great Depression and the Second World War.

How his grandfather managed to get to Australia was a mystery. Perhaps he had worked his passage aboard a ship. He was a carpenter by trade. Ross thought he must have been brave enough to leave his city for what would have been a strange country in the southern hemisphere.

When he got to Australia, he went to inland Queensland, where the only job available was as a jackaroo, an Australian version of a cowboy. Perhaps he was the original Pommy Jackaroo! This meant being in the saddle for long periods in one of the driest places in the country. At times, he must have sweated a bucket. Ross once was in that area and understood how the heat could get to someone. He knew a good hat and filled water bottles were essential to survival. He couldn't imagine going from a cold city like London and facing the heat found in cattle country, Queensland. His grandfather must have been a tough fellow when he was young.

When the First World War broke out, he could return to England to join the army or the Australian Light Horse. He chose the Australian Light Horse, little knowing he wouldn't be required to do much horse riding. After basic training, he boarded a ship, thinking he would go to France. He ended up in Egypt for further training. Then he was sent to Gallipoli, in Turkey. After surviving Gallipoli, he was sent to France, where he received wounds that would take him out of the war. His wounds were so bad that it was thought he would die. Somehow, he managed to recover with the help of a nurse who had previously been a barmaid.

He married this nurse, and they journeyed to Australia together to start a new life. Despite carrying shrapnel from the war within him, he could use the carpentry skills he had to create work for himself. They settled in Sydney, New South Wales, rather than Queensland, since he felt the cooler climate better suited his wife. Ross reasoned that his grandmother must have been brave to leave London for Australia. His grandmother's sister had travelled to Canada for a better life, which Ross also found courageous. His grandparents had three children, two boys and a girl. The girl was Ross's mother.

Ross wondered if the system would have been happy with him going to some foreign country and getting himself blown up. But would he have been that lucky? Instant death didn't always happen as it did on some television shows of the 1960s, in most of the movies of that era, and earlier on.

In reality, a soldier might lie, bleeding and in pain, on a battlefield for a long time before death takes him. Additionally, even with proper medical care, not all injuries result in a full recovery. His grandfather was proof of that. The American television show *Boardwalk Empire* stressed this point with a man who had come back from World War I with such a horrific facial injury that he wears a half mask to appear as normal as possible.

Ross could not recall any kids pretending to be soldiers fighting the Viet Cong. Maybe the bloodshed and the confusion that were televised were too real. It took Ross over a decade to understand what was happening in that country and why the war could not be won. Australian troops pulled out before the Americans decided they had had enough.

He enjoyed *The Dam Busters* and *The Battle of Britain*, the British war films he saw growing up. He liked the ingenuity that went into making a bomb that bounced. He enjoyed seeing Spitfires and Hurricanes in action. In *The Battle of Britain*, the viewer was shown what could happen to one's face, not to mention other parts of one's body, while exiting a burning Spitfire or Hurricane. This was a rare glimpse at the time of the true horrors of war.

Reason tended to triumph over brute force in the first few decades of the British television series Doctor Who. Ross liked the show until the Woke took over and ruined everything. It was a sign for him that nothing good could last forever.

Regarding comic books, Ross was not very interested in war or cowboys. The war and cowboy comics of the 1960s and early 1970s were just too simplistic to stomach. They were all unrealistic in genres that should have had much more realism. He liked science fiction and superheroes. At least with science fiction and superheroes, there was no need for pretence at realism. He later learned that the Comics Code Authority, a form of censorship, weakened the war and cowboy comics of the 1960s and early 1970s.

Before the Second World War, artists and writers developed superheroes; the best tended to be American. Superman was the first.

When the United States entered World War II, so did its superheroes. Characters from the stable that would one day be Marvel included Captain America, the Sub-Mariner, the Destroyer, and the android Human Torch.

Ross liked that the Sub-Mariner was born in the waters of the Antarctic. This made him the first superhero he knew of born in the southern hemisphere, his half of the world. He was shocked when, in the 21st Century, a movie maker depicted the submariner as either from South America or Central America instead of Antarctica. It was a blatant disregard for the original illustrator and writer. What horrible political correctness and woke in action!

The best artist of the 20th Century was Jack Kirby of Captain America fame, who worked for many comic book companies, including Marvel and DC. Other artists from the 1940s were Bill Everett (Sub-Mariner) and Carl Burgos (The Human Torch). In the 1970s, Gene Colan created some fantastic artwork for *Daredevil* and *Tomb of Dracula*.

The superhero craze petered out in America in the early 1950s. War and horror became popular. Atlas published some gritty war comics during this period, but Ross did not learn about them until the early 21st Century.

In the mid-1950s, the Comics Code Authority rocked the American comic book industry. Any comic book with horror in the title was out, and war comics had to be toned down. By the 1970s, however, the Comics Code Authority had been weakened so that Marvel could publish the *Tomb of Dracula*.

There wasn't much of an Australian comic industry during the Second World War, and what there was struggled when, in the 1960s, American comic books and English comic papers flooded the country. Australia had some excellent artists, but no comic book company could adjust to the wants and needs of the 1960s comic book-buying public. Frew, the only Australian company that stayed afloat in those times, continued to publish the American comic strip *The Phantom*.

Ross knew that efforts in the 1980s to create Australian superheroes could have been more successful. It suffered mainly due to poor packaging and a lack of financial backing. In the 1980s, you couldn't expect to put out a new superhero comic that wasn't in colour and expect it to sell.

There was also a certain amount of cultural cringe in which many Australians looked to what was happening overseas, ignoring what was being done locally. Ross recalled the Australian movie *Mad Max* as a trendsetter, as the French and other nationalities loved it.

A horror anthology comic book came out in Australia in the 1980s. It had top-quality art by Steve Carter and Des Waterman, but it also needed to be in colour. Unfortunately, there wasn't enough money for it to be in full colour. The era when new comic books could be in black and white had long passed. Later, horror comics were published in Australia in colour, but major distribution was often complex.

In the 1970s and 1980s, the British tended to favour hard-hitting science fiction with dark humour in their comic papers, such as the adventures of Judge Dredd, who was both an arresting officer and an executioner when it came to violent crime. Some of Judge Dredd's adventures were eventually published in American comic books.

During the early 21st Century, American comic book companies tried various ways to expand their readership. Going Woke was not a good idea. The result was that more Americans, Australians, and British readers deserted Marvel and D.C. Japanese comics in English took up the slack. There were also more readers going for Dark Horse and other comic publishers. Whoever could produce comics without the politically correct preaching or Woke nonsense could make a killing in the marketplace.

CHAPTER SIX

Who the Hell Are You?

Ross Martin did wonder who he was and what he could ever make out of himself. Perhaps there was good raw material to work with, but that was about it. He had two hands, two feet and two of everything he needed to get somewhere in society. He wasn't born rich and couldn't see how to become wealthy since his dad wasn't well-off. He felt, at times, that he was a small man in a world that wanted him to be tiny, mouse-like, and be no trouble. This was the system in action.

Schools catered for those pupils who caused strife. Lessons were disrupted while they were being sorted out. They got detention, but that didn't matter. Being put on suspension was like a holiday to them and a headache for their parents. In private schools, they could be shown the door for good, but not in public schools. This was one reason private schools were prized by parents who could afford to send their children to such places. Those who didn't want to learn or could not do so could only be in the public school system.

This catering to the scumbags in public schools was especially true when the use of the cane was banned. How best to keep order then? Was corporal punishment such a great idea anyway? Ross wondered about this as a high school student. He thought the cane was demeaning, but he knew it had a long history in education. Later, he was to learn about students turning on teachers and getting violent with them when the use of the cane had been discontinued decades ago.

He understood that once students had left high school, it wasn't necessary, right or wrong, to keep them in line with any form of physical punishment. Either you'd learn in college or university, or soon be out with no degree and a less promising future. That had suited Ross fine. This did not mean, though, that he didn't get sloshed on booze some weekends or had problems with specific courses he had taken.

Music was one area he couldn't get into at primary or high school because of his poor math skills. He thought he would give it a college try, but quickly discovered he was too far behind other students who had studied it in primary and high school. He reluctantly got out of it, sighing deeply that it was still not for him. *Those bastard teachers in primary and high school stole any chance I had,* he told himself and knew he was right, but being correct didn't change anything. He had to conclude that certain forms of learning were never meant to be, though he thought he might try one last time when he was in retirement.

Ross was not going to be a star athlete. However, this was acceptable to him, as he would experiment with sports to make friends. Taking it too seriously just wasn't in him. His cousins did that, and they were welcome to do so.

He also couldn't see himself seriously barracking for this or that rugby team. If asked who he did barrack for by someone well into it, he would favour Saint George because it was his dad's favourite team. Thus, having Saint George as backup got him out of a few awkward moments.

He saw his future as a writer. The problem was that many others also saw their future in that direction. So, was he any good? He thought so, especially when he got an article in a magazine or a story in an anthology. He had his fair share of rejections, but decided not to let them drag him down.

Ross remembered being a group member who worked, off and on, for the railways and buses. He talked, at times, too fancy for some of his co-workers, but they got to know him and liked him. For the better part of eight years, they were like family. At the end of every year, the boss provided a banquet somewhere.

He worked at times with an elderly man who always smelled of tobacco. The fellow had wanted to retire via his super, but most of it was wiped out when the banks in the USA went belly up. It was the domino effect. What hurt USA banking inevitably hurt shares in US companies, and what was considered a blue-chip investment was not as safe as it should have been. Additionally, banks in the UK and Australia were adversely affected by the issues in the USA.

In the 1960s, Ross's dad was a foreman in a factory. One of the workers was a woman in hiding from her brutal husband. She was referred to as Lady M. One Christmas, she gave Ross a present: a book about Australia. Ross and his father did not know what had happened to her after she had left the factory. It was hoped her husband hadn't caught up with her.

Ross also remembered his dad telling him about Aborigines working in that factory. He said they were good workers, but preferred only to be there six months out of the year. His dad always did his best to accommodate them in this. They weren't any trouble, and his dad could always rely on them being on time for work. Ross never found out what these Aborigines thought about his dad or what they did at that factory. While working in the country, Ross had the opportunity to work with Aborigines. He found they were all right.

Art appealed to Ross, but he wasn't taught much about it in primary or high school. He got the impression that those not good at Maths didn't deserve a complete education.

He learned about traditional and otherwise art in college through 19th-century American and British literature, and later from his artistic friends. 19th-century tales and poetry were illustrated in the books he read, and gave a taste of what it was like to view art back then. He was particularly taken with the Pre-Raphaelites and their fascination for redheaded women. He especially liked the painting of a female lake spirit. Years later, he saw a television mini-series on the life and times of these energetic and wayward artists. In some ways, they reminded him of the Australian artists he knew.

CHAPTER SEVEN

Angels and Demons

Ross had his demons. One Easter, he would have cheerfully blown up his kindergarten. He didn't want to harm anyone. He just figured if it blew up, he would have to go to another kindergarten that would hopefully be more friendly towards left-handed people like himself. He thought everything would be all right if it blew up during the holidays and no one was caught. Of course, being a child, it was all a pipe dream and nothing more.

In later years, he had to wonder about teenagers in the USA who get their hands on firearms and shoot so-called fellow students they detest. He understood that teenagers in the USA were more divided into groups than teenagers in Australia and elsewhere. He couldn't remember the athletes being treated differently from anyone else in his high school, for example, how they were treated like gold in the USA. If he were to gun down anyone in his high school, it would have been the idiots who disrupted lessons with the same tired old routines.

Then, in the 21st Century, there was that maniac kid in England who decided to stab as many young girls as he possibly could. It was lucky for him that there wasn't a death penalty for what he had done, though there were people who would have gladly reinstated it just for him.

One time when Ross went camping with his dad, he looked into the coals of a campfire, watching them go from glowing red to black. Did this make him a pyromaniac? No. His dad taught him to put out the fire before calling it a night. His fascination for the flames did not extend to criminal activity, but he did wonder about those who did lean in that direction.

Viewing any human being as pure good or evil was a profound mistake many men have made over the centuries. The angel bit concerns wishful thinking and how the system operates. In old age, Ross knew better but had still gone through that phase where most women were either angelic or demonic.

There was a psychologist on YouTube in the 21st Century who came out with the reason women married thugs. They wanted protection from other thugs. He couldn't imagine Glenda, his lady love, needing his protection, but she had it if required. It did, however, anger him toward sports freaks, and there was still a twinge of anger in him toward his cousins, who couldn't believe it when they saw him dancing with a beautiful woman.

From an early age, he understood that his sister, Kate, was neither all good nor all bad. At times, he had trouble translating this knowledge into an understanding of other females. In this, he was painfully naïve and would pay for his naivety. His mother should have also been evidence that women were as human as he was, even if, in some instances, they had different wants and needs.

According to the Bible, evil began for humans when they consumed the forbidden fruit in the Garden of Eden. A serpent tempted Eve to take the fruit and share it with Adam. Ross Martin was told by a Methodist preacher that Adam was reluctant to take a bite of this fruit, but Eve talked him into it. If she was going to get into trouble with God, she didn't want to be alone.

Eve and women have been tainted by this first wrongdoing ever since. Was a female demon involved? Did this female demon talk the serpent into having a chat with Eve? Possibly. The big one after that was Cane slaying Able. What followed was a lot of begetting, which didn't make much sense to Ross. Generations of humanity seemed to ebb and flow without much comment.

Ross could understand why Cane was mad at both Able and God. He had worked hard in the field to get his offering together, whereas Able simply slew animals. As far as Ross was concerned, God should never have praised one brother without praising the other, especially if both were doing things to please him.

In college, during medieval studies, Ross found out why the forbidden fruit for the British and others became the apple. For artists, it had to be something identifiable that could be seen in churches and cathedrals. It might have been something else if not for the Norman conquest. In Saxon times and the Saxon chronicles, the word apple meant the same thing as the Norman-French word fruit. After the Normans took over, fruit dominated, and the apple became what it is today: a type of fruit. But did someone look up the Saxon account of the Eden story, see the tree referred to as an apple tree, and say that's it, from now on, the forbidden fruit was a type of apple? Ross could imagine just how that could have happened.

Scientists had it; Ross knew from a television program that if the Garden of Eden had ever existed, it was probably in Africa or an oasis in the Middle East. The real forbidden fruit might have been a date if it were an oasis.

Ross was once told a legend about a 17th-century pope. The end of days was coming, and the Church had to be ready for it when it did happen. This pope decided that recreating King Solomon's temple, which was said to be made of solid gold, was the way to go. It would please God.

This structure would require a significant amount of precious metal. The demand for gold thus rose. Ultimately, the temple was not built, and people continued to wait for the end of everything.

Could a temple made of solid gold stand? Was Solomon's temple made of the stuff? Ross doubted it could hold its weight since gold is both a heavy metal and soft. He thought someone might try it if the gold was available, and the pope was keen on such a project.

If Solomon's temple had been made of gold, it would have been made of gold plate over wood or some other metal, which, to Ross, made more sense. The Ancient Egyptians had the secret of gold plating, so why not Solomon's people?

In the 17th Century, the Spanish extracted significant gold from South America. It was enough to devalue that glistening metal, but not all of it was pure. Pirates such as Sir Francis Drake plundered Spanish vessels for gold and whatever else they could find of value.

The king of Spain got sick of his vessels being attacked and sent an armada to invade England. The invasion was not successful. The lighter English vessels were able to maneuver better in English Channel waters. Additionally, there were issues with the Spanish barrels on board their ships splitting. One Spanish ship went aground in Ireland. Those Spanish sailors had hoped that the Irish would aid them. Unfortunately for them, they had landed in a part of Ireland that was pro-England and thus were either killed or arrested.

From his college studies, Ross understood that many people had misconceptions about the Spanish Inquisition. It was never about persecuting the Jews. There had been a proclamation from the king and queen of Spain giving the Jews two years in which to leave Spain. Any who remained after that time would be executed. The alternative to leaving was to become a Christian. Some chose to become Christians, and as a result, the belief developed that not all new Christians had given up their old religion. A Jew could not be accused of heresy, but this could and did happen to new Christians. There were new Christians who were put to the Inquisition simply because they were better at their trade than people who had been Christians longer. And there were also men and women of just about every background accused of witchcraft by members of their community keen on being rid of them.

Throughout human history, Ross understood, it was made easy by the Church and other organisations to either think of women as demonic or angelic. This came from the Catholic Church being ruled over by men, many of them forbidden to have sexual relations with women and thus having little to do with the opposite sex. Additionally, the Church could potentially reap a financial gain if an elderly woman with property were accused of witchcraft, and subsequently, Church authorities could seize the property.

Ross was aware of the desire to have angelic women in his life. The appeal of rejecting the notion that any woman might indeed be demonic was there. Were Jem and her mother exceptions? He might have once thought so. As he grew older, he could see them as bad, but in a very human way. He didn't believe demons were snobs like Jem and her mother, but he could be wrong. What, after all, was a demon? From what he read in college, it was a creature that brought out the worst in others. Both Jem and her mother qualified. They brought out the worst in Ross, and he knew it.

There were times when he imagined saving a pretty girl from a fire, getting run over by a car, or being hit on the head by a falling brick from a building about to collapse. From the early 1960s to the mid-1970s, most movies, television shows, comic strips, and comic books from the USA featured women rescued from either villains or nature gone awry. The women tended to be angelic and were deserving of salvation. Moreover, they often tend to sprain their ankles in novels, movies, and television.

In the 19th Century, in fiction, women were in danger of fainting. This may not have been so ridiculous if one realised, as did Ross, that corsets restrict the breathing of some women and thus fainting was both possible and reasonable.

Ross had to smile at how the 1960s Batman television series portrayed women who were costumed and villainous. Batman saw them as misguided and thus in need of help. He didn't see them as responsible for their actions, even if they enjoyed wickedness. This was a mockery of the naivety about women that had been so prevalent in the comics, especially in the USA, since the Comics Code Authority had been instigated.

In the 1992 movie *Batman Returns*, Michelle Pfeiffer played a Catwoman pushed into the role by an unscrupulous businessman who, instead of killing her as intended, made her over into a female predator.

From his college studies, Ross understood that the way English men of the middle to upper classes were educated in the 19th and early 20th Centuries tended to alienate them from the opposite sex. This was also true for women. What happens when all your schooling is either boys only or girls only, and you never meet up with young members of the opposite sex except on the holidays? Ross imagined it caused some confusion.

He thought 1901 French postcards of naked women riding pushbikes came into vogue from the desire of adolescent boys throughout Europe proper, as well as the British Empire, to see a nude woman. He imagined that such postcards, if they were originals, would be worth quite a bit to collectors by the 21st Century. He also recalled seeing copies of English postcards first issued in the 1950s, which contained jokes about what might be appealing at the local beach resort. Such naughtiness was not for the politically correct or the Woke folk.

Tongue-in-cheek humour that pointed out the silly was evident in the British Carry-on movies. It was also featured in The Paul Hogan

Show, a popular Australian program in the 1970s. In later years, The Paul Hogan Show was accused of being anti-women. Ross knew this to be untrue. If anything, the show took its comedy from misconceptions about women that often led to the stooge getting into trouble.

In the 1990s, Ross had an artist friend who believed the world would be better if more women were in positions of power. After his time in the office with that Japanese woman, Ross knew the fellow was wrong. Power could and did consume women much like it did men, if not precisely in the same way. Put women instead of men in high positions, and there might be a change, but the results would be the same. Ross thought British Prime Minister Margaret Thatcher was an excellent example of this. He knew of a Scotsman who had worked for the railways in New South Wales, who positively hated her and what she had done to the UK.

Ross encountered people who believed there wasn't a class system in the USA or Australia. "Just because it has to do with money rather than land or titles doesn't mean it doesn't exist," one of his college lecturers told him, and she was right. He could see how wealth, or lack thereof, had to be a factor in who he was eligible to go out with and who he was not.

One of his earlier mistakes may have been asking a young woman whose parents were wealthier than his own. She lacked interest and acted as if he had insulted her.

Ross, at college, knew the sons of wealthy landowners who tended to dress down rather than up. In summer, they were often seen in faded T-shirts and jeans. The giveaway with them was the snazzy four-wheel drives they owned. Nothing else about them suggested that their parents were doing much better than okay, but that was more than enough.

Religions other than Christianity also played a role in how women were perceived and treated. There was a documentary on television that Ross found disturbing. It involved a Muslim family residing in Pakistan. The son, who had immigrated to Australia, was visiting his parents in their small town in Pakistan. The program revealed that his mother had not left her husband's home in decades. She could not even travel across the road without a male family escort if she were to leave his house. Her only role was to make children and look after them for the greater good. Ross thought her life was terrible and hoped, for her sake, she had never been an intelligent woman.

Were all Muslim families in Pakistan like that? Ross hoped that was not the case. One lousy family, he realised, should not condemn a culture or a religion. Even so, according to YouTube, in the 21st Century, there were Pakistani rape gangs in the UK that the people there couldn't seem to do anything about.

Ross was against female circumcision being practised in Australia because he thought it was barbaric. It was often done when the child was reaching womanhood, and, though strictly not a Muslim thing, it was part of cultures that were Muslim-based. It was painful and of no benefit to the young woman.

It was true Ross had been circumcised when he was very young, but he had no memory of the operation. It was performed at a time when it was common practice in Australian hospitals, and the person being circumcised didn't have to be Jewish. Ross, however, was against male circumcision because a slip of the blade while it was being done would mean the male child would have problems with his maleness for the rest of his life. This didn't happen very often, but it did happen. Ross saw a documentary about it.

CHAPTER EIGHT

Civilisation

The system was part of the civilisation Ross belonged to, and it was something he could only defeat in old age. Others, such as his brother, had managed it much earlier.

Ross understood the system was all about protecting the sheep from the wolves, and he, being a white male, was considered by the system and those who supported it to be a wolf. Even changing his clothing did not change him into a sheep. What he wanted was very wolf-like, and that he couldn't deny. Once he got what he wanted and married her, he figured he'd no longer be a wolf but one of the sheep, and, after that, the system wouldn't be against him but, in some twisted way, on his side. Could he stand the idea of the system being for him rather than against him? He thought he could.

The civilisation he was part of had its benefits. The government, until 2023, ensured that no one starved and that most people had a roof over their heads. Charities, such as the Salvation Army, cared for anyone the government couldn't or wouldn't help.

But how do you define civilisation? Ross described it as accomplishing something that the few or the one cannot perform, but many people can. Many marvels came out of Western-style civilisation, from ships able to cross oceans to weapons capable of killing thousands, if not millions, of people in one go, such as the atomic bomb. In 1969, the United States successfully landed men on the moon.

Town and city planners in the UK, Australia, New Zealand, and the USA kept some green areas vacant for the sanity of those living in such locales. Seattle in the USA was a great example of doing this right. Sydney, Australia, was also a marvellous example, as was Wollongong, south of Sydney.

Ross thought the Botanic Garden in Wollongong, near the university, was better than the one in Sydney. He didn't have much interest in flowers, but where there were flowering plants, there was wildlife. He liked the satin bower birds at Wollongong's Botanic Garden near the bird bath. The males look regal in their blue, and the females look like they could take you on in their green. He considered the Botanic Garden in Darwin also well worth a second visit. The plants and birds had to deal not only with the dry season but also with the wet.

Efforts were made to avoid war, but they didn't always succeed. In the 20th Century, there wasn't a decade in which men in uniform from Australia were not fighting people living somewhere else. At the start of the 21st Century, it looked like the trend established in the 20th Century would continue.

Were Western-style civilisations doomed? Had they run their course like other great civilisations, and were they now coming to an end? Some thought Western-style civilisations had an expiry date. In the 1980s, scholars at the college where Ross was claimed that such civilisations were already in their economic death throes. Ross discovered that no one could agree on what could replace them other than rule by dictatorship.

Electronic computers have been part of Western civilisation since the late 19th Century.

Ross understood that during the Second World War, computers were used by the British and Americans to help decipher enemy codes, thereby helping to win battles. Back then, a computer could take up an entire room, if not a whole floor.

He remembered the science fiction movie *The Invisible Boy* (1957), in which a whole room was dedicated to a supercomputer. Other movies also showed computers as massive. For example, in the 1983 film *War Games*, a large computer comes close to triggering World War III.

From the 1980s onward, most people living in the United States, the United Kingdom, and Australia had private computers capable of linking up with the evolving Internet. Ross was one of them. Over time, these personal computers became less bulky and more sophisticated. They expanded Western-style civilisation the way television had a generation earlier and, even earlier still, radio.

Ross remembered a Christmas party in the 1980s when a photo of a Playboy model was downloaded onto a computer. It took half an hour. A decade later, it would take much less time and a matter of seconds by the 21st Century. Still, in the 1980s, getting the photo was astounding, even if the wait for it was a trifle long.

Did China kick-start Western civilisation, and was it prepared to take over in the 21st Century? Ross knew from his studies that the Chinese once had this impressive and expanding civilisation. Then, for reasons known best to themselves and possibly the Mongols, they became increasingly insular, giving Western powers their chance to grow.

By the 19th Century, the Western powers and Japan were ready to invade China and divide that part of the world. This did not happen, but it was close. Ross was unsure why it didn't occur.

In the 20th Century, Japan's invasion of China contributed to the outbreak of the Second World War. The Japanese needed oil to sustain their attack on the Chinese, and the Western powers were reluctant to supply it. This created hostilities that resulted in a Japanese attack on Singapore and Hawaii.

Ross understood the importance of the Battle of Midway from his studies. During this battle, the Japanese had the opportunity to impede America's ability to wage war in the Pacific. Instead, the Japanese fleet was severely mauled, and so the Japanese Imperialists could not win the war they had started.

In the 21st Century, there was talk as to why the atomic bombs were ever used at all. To Ross, it came down to efforts to save the lives of American soldiers who would have otherwise been lost in an invasion of mainland Japan. There were those in the 21st Century who thought the use of those atomic bombs was to prevent the Russian military from swooping in and taking over Japan. Ross thought this to be woke nonsense. Anything to make the Americans, in some way, look bad.

Ross understood that Britain once had a vast empire. Two world wars later, it struggled to keep any of it together. India had to be relinquished, and eventually, Malaya became the Republic of Malaysia, gaining independence. By the 1960s, the South Pacific could no longer be guarded by Royal Navy vessels. An alliance with the United States was then formed with the Australian government to protect regional interests.

Was the empire helpful to the average person living in Britain in the early 20th Century? Ross didn't think so. It was okay for the elite, but pockets of poverty could be found in London and other major cities in Britain. Ross's grandfather, on his mother's side, had come from a London pocket where breakfast, growing up, consisted of bread together with dripping from the previous night's meal. Jam was too expensive.

Ross's mother remembered Empire Day, and there were photos of picnics where people waved the British flag. Even after the Second World War, many Australians felt a sense of belonging to the British Empire.

France, Ross learned, fared worse than Britain after those two world wars. In the 1950s, Vietnam was lost to the French. The USA made efforts in the 1960s to ensure Vietnam didn't fall into communist hands. War ensued, and a decade later, the Americans left Vietnam. Ross remembered discussions in college about the domino effect and whether it was a real phenomenon. Would enough countries have fallen to communism and thus put Australia in danger if the USA and other countries hadn't stepped in to take on the communists?

After the First World War, the USA became a financial giant among nations. It loaned capital to numerous countries, including Australia. When Wall Street in New York collapsed, it led to the Great Depression, which affected numerous countries, including Australia.

What did any of this have to do with Ross? His parents grew up in those depression years and did it tough. Toys tended to be homemade, and kids played in the streets and open fields. The food was plain and simple. Apples and potatoes were cheap. The Rabbito would come around selling freshly killed rabbits. In his late teens, Ross's father would hunt for rabbits with a rifle in places such as Hills End. A successful hunt and kill meant good tucker for the family, at the price of a bullet.

For decades, rabbit meat was the cheapest. Then, the government decided to use poison to eradicate the wild rabbits, and as a result, rabbits became more expensive.

Ross recalled meals at home in the 1960s consisting of stewed rabbit with carrots, onions, and dumplings. The rabbit was bought from the local butcher. Then, rabbits in the butcher shops became scarce, so rabbits for supper ended.

Ross's grandfather on his father's side struggled to keep a roof over the heads of his wife and children and had a stroke in doing so.

Back then, there was more community spirit, and the radio was essential to life. *Pick-a-box* was a favourite program, and there were *The Adventures of Speed Gordon* (it should have been Flash, as in the American comic strip, but the name was altered for Australian consumption because Flash evoked images of people running naked).

Australia eventually caught up in getting television. At first, sets were too expensive for the average consumer. Hence, radio dominated the airwaves for much longer than it might have otherwise.

On holidays in May, Ross often had no television, but there was always the radio to listen to if that was what he wanted to do. He remembered listening to *Sammy Sparrow* first thing in the morning as he got ready to go fishing with his dad.

Ross discovered, through research, that the Wall Street collapse of 1929 was not the first to occur in the USA, but because it affected much of the world this time, it was the most devastating. The Second World War arrived, and rearming the USA meant what was thought to be, on this occasion, only a temporary end to financial woes. When the war ended, however, the Great Depression did not resume either in the USA or Australia. There was, however, a minor economic downturn in the USA that could have signalled the resumption of the Great Depression, but thankfully, it failed to do so. To this day, Ross still understands that economists are puzzled by this incident. Some said the air of optimism in the 1950s did the trick. It could also have been the new plastics that came on the market.

From the Second World War to the 1960s, Americans were encouraged to buy government bonds and stamps. Perhaps this also stopped the return of the Great Depression. Television shows such as *Mr Ed and Adventures of Superman* had cast members speak out in favour of these bonds and stamps.

1989, the Cold War between the United States and the Soviet Union ended. One reason for this was the sad state of the Russian economy. Russians could no longer keep up with the arms race. Despite the end of the Cold War, the Russian economy remained in disarray for another decade.

Looking back on his life, Ross noted he had spent some time in college in the 1980s learning about the world and how it had come to be in its current condition. He felt that communism, the Russian style, had had its day by then, but not the Chinese form, which was more flexible. The Chinese had learned from what had happened to the Russians.

Forms of communism had been festering in universities in the USA, the UK and Australia and would come to light as Woke in the early 21st Century. Woke must have seemed to many a good idea. Caring about people is never bad, except when you do it wrong.

Ross understood that, for over thirty years, businessmen and women in Western-style countries had glorified making lots of money off the poorer Third World countries, such as Indonesia, and the poor living in their own countries. From the 1980s onward, he noted that not one item of clothing he owned didn't originate from some Third World country.

Looking at an article in a history book, Ross realised that in Australia in the 1900s, there wasn't a stitch of clothing worn by the average, well-to-do businessman working in Australia that was made in Australia. He observed that Italian suits and shoes were the go.

Was the growing dependence on Third World goods harming the West? Ross thought so from the 1980s onward, but because he was not a businessman, he couldn't see any other option than to keep buying from these Third World countries. There seemed to be no way for factories and companies in Australia and elsewhere in the West to compete with the low prices of goods offered by places such as Bangladesh, Indonesia, India, and Pakistan. Where wages and living conditions were low, prices could also be low. Only in scientific knowledge and electronics did the Western-style countries hold sway, and that, in the 21st Century, was being challenged by China.

Would the Chinese be content with buying bits and pieces of Australia, or would they someday make a military grab for the whole country? In the early 21st Century, Ross thought this grab for the lot was possible. If the grab occurred, would the USA intervene militarily on behalf of Australians or impose trade restrictions on China that are unlikely to be effective?

Was there a possibility that China would invade Japan in the future? Ross didn't think so, though he thought it was more likely than an invasion by the Chinese of Australia. He thought there was a strong possibility that China would annex Taiwan. If they attempted it, would the USA intervene? Ross didn't think so.

The wild card was North Korea. Would the leader of that country do something foolish and start the Third World War? Ross didn't know. He knew from the news that people living in South Korea lived better lives than those in the North. Farmers in the North were said to do it especially tough. Ross remembered a television documentary about a supermarket in North Korea with Western goods. Few North Koreans could afford to shop there because these goods were expensive.

Meanwhile, some people in Indonesia thought Australia should have always been part of a more extraordinary Indonesia. Ross encountered them during his studies. He knew that people from Indonesia had visited parts of Australia before Lieutenant Cook's arrival on the east coast. Before Cook, there were also British pirate vessels at home on the west coast, so Britain had a tentative claim to Australia even before Cook's voyage. Then, there was the French claiming part of New South Wales. There were Japanese pearl divers in Australian waters in the 19th Century who were allowed to work there for a limited time but were not allowed to live in Australia permanently. Of course, Australian Aborigines have lived on the land much longer than anyone in Europe, Indonesia or Japan.

What did any of this mean? Ross was content to think of himself as an Australian since his father and his father's father had been born in Australia. It was his country.

CHAPTER NINE

Art

For Ross Martin, art provided a sense of freedom from the system. It seemed in art that the monster couldn't claw him.

To him, the leading art form of the 20th Century had been the American comic book. It remained there in the 21st Century, although it struggled against Japanese manga.

Ross knew that everyone past ten had their definition of art. Even the experts couldn't always agree on what it was or how it should come to be. He knew that the First World War was so horrific that the paintings that resulted from it were dynamic and boldly different from what had come before. He remembered seeing a German image of a man with no legs sitting on a street corner selling pencils. He was wrapped up warm as if it were a cold winter morning. It was an ugly yet compelling image.

During the Second World War, there were propaganda images of what the Japanese would do if they were successful in invading Australia. One painting Ross remembered seeing as part of an art exhibit in Sydney had this young woman being menaced by a Japanese soldier. The Japanese had a bayonet stuck on their rifle.

Art got muddy for Ross when it came to the so-called modern stuff. What did this have to do with the system? Perhaps traditional art was an acceptance of it, and contemporary art was another way of defying it. Either way, Ross only sometimes found modern examples that fit his taste or understanding.

Ross learned of a male latrine displayed in a German art museum through his college studies. It had been there from the 1920s onwards. When Ross asked one of his artist friends why, he was told it did count as art. "How?" pushed Ross. "The artist exhibiting it didn't make it. The latrine was manufactured in a factory. He, whoever he was, just took it from somewhere, probably the tip, and put it on display. Apart from being an eye-opener to women as to how men pee standing up, what use is it?" Ross's artist friend told him this artist also painted, which seemed to be a reason to believe the piece was art. How the latrine, and quite possibly the artist, survived Hitler's reign of terror on the modern art world was beyond his understanding. Maybe Hitler didn't care, one way or the other, for latrines on display.

In the 1980s, before attending college, Ross took a class at a workers' education centre, where he was introduced to art by visionaries such as Paul Klee. He didn't care at all for Klee's efforts in this book, which illustrated his work, presented in black and white photos. However, when he saw Klee's flying horse in colour, he was deeply moved and impressed. The colour made all the difference. There was also Claude Monet, the master of light and Matisse with his primitivism.

In summer, sand sculptures were created in Bondi and Cronulla. Some were impressive. One that caught Ross's eye at Cronulla was a seaplane about to take off. These efforts would have eventually fallen apart except for the photos taken of them, which were placed in magazines, newspapers, and on the internet. The camera to the rescue.

An artist once used a lot of white cloth to cover part of Sydney's headland. Photos were taken, and the results were proclaimed as art. Of course, it was only temporary, as the cloth had to be removed for the wildlife and sightseers, but it was still eye-catching. Ordinary bricks were once placed in a pyramid on a raised platform, signifying Ross knew not what. Maybe they were a salute to Ancient Egypt.

Around the same time, Ross instantly disliked these wimpy paintings of the Sydney Harbour Bridge in an art gallery. They were all in light pastels, denying the bridge's strength and its importance to life in Sydney. The bridge had been built when Australians needed a symbol of power.

Was photography art? Ross liked to think so. He found that getting the shots of birds and other wildlife he wanted took time and effort. He compared his photography to minimalism. A minimalist artist sets out to draw a woman with ten strokes of a thin brush with black ink. It takes ten seconds to do so. This does not, however, include the weeks and possibly months of planning those ten strokes and the times on paper when he didn't quite get what he wanted; he didn't quite get it right.

There was a photographer who gained fame for his nude photographs. Hundreds of people of all shapes and sizes would pose naked for him against well-known European landmarks. Ross wondered if he would ever want to be such a cameraman. It would be daring work. It would also be him poking his tongue out at the system. He figured the system hated nudity.

Ross once saw Japanese kites and lanterns on display in Sydney. They were art because they had vibrantly coloured dragons, tigers, and robots painted on them.

People claimed cooking was an art. Ross didn't get this in his formative years, but once he became familiar with Japanese-style food preparation, he could see where that could be a possibility.

While working for the railways, he encountered electrical boxes painted in various styles. One had these books flying off into the sky, their pages open to the imagined wind. This was at North Wollongong.

Ross, after college, wrote short vampire stories, some of which ended up in print. He also had a minor success with a yarn about a mummy rising from the dead. He thought of writing about his past, but gave it up as something very few punters would be interested in reading.

CHAPTER TEN

The Pagan Past

While in college, Ross Martin encountered many references to paganism. He figured the system would frown on it. Paganism harked back to freedoms long lost and unlikely to be recovered. Even so, some forms of paganism still exist, but for how long, Ross didn't know. Every year, they were attacked on social media. He couldn't imagine the politically correct or the Woke caring much for them.

There was the idea that people always believed in something and were not just waiting for a Christian preacher to appear in their village to give them the good word. Some still found the pre-Christian world offensive, and being offended was what both the politically correct and the Woke were all about.

Were European pagans sacrificing humans to their gods? This was something Christians tended to climb aboard on. Some did so, which was terrible, while others did not and were against such a practice. Ross understood the need not to bung the pagan world into one neat package. Different tribes had different ways. Paganism had been around for many centuries and had undergone significant evolution.

Ross had seen paintings of young and old women dancing naked around a fire. Then there was the art of Norman Lindsay. His Blue

Mountains paintings and sculptures remain defiant in the face of those who would ban the nude and the magical. Lindsay once tutored the woman who came to be known as the Witch of Kings Cross. Ross thought her paintings were overly simplistic, but Lindsay's were not.

A walk-through of Lindsay's Garden and home in the Blue Mountains was always inspirational. He had been there a couple of times with his sister. On such visits, they had scones with clotted cream and jam, fresh from the oven, and Earl Grey tea with milk and sugar.

Even in Lindsay's day, it seemed that not everyone forced into becoming a Christian wanted to follow that path. Lindsay saw wonder in his world, and that was what he painted and sculpted. It appeared to Ross that certain Christians were only happy with what could be discovered after death. *No one knows what happens to us after we die*, thought Ross one day at Lindsay's place. *But we can always find a better way to live.*

Ross was taken with the film *Sirens* (1994), which is about Lindsay's models and his art. However, when he talked to the woman in charge of Lindsay's home, she told him the film was racier than Lindsay's life had been. He felt a little disappointed. He liked a painting where maidens descend to Earth and are intrigued by the men they find there.

Reflecting on his past thoughts, Ross understood, from his college studies, that Christianity had benefited both the Saxon and Norman lords in governing kingdoms such as England. The Christian faith could keep the lower classes from rebelling if the belief could be maintained that a better world awaited them after death if they behaved themselves.

Going back even further, the Romans sought to maintain their empire, believing it could be achieved through the power of religion. The first attempt was to create a sun god, which failed. The second was Christianity, which also failed to preserve the empire's integrity.

The Romans, or their servants, first introduced the Christian message to the people of Britain, but how this differed from later interpretations of Christianity isn't always straightforward. Did they have a Bible to go by, or was it word of mouth?

Despite the best efforts of Roman emperors, the Roman Empire gradually disintegrated. Rome itself went into ruin after being sacked numerous times by barbarians, but the notion of a central faith pulling everything together persisted. The children of those who had brought the empire down took up the idea. The result was the creation of a new Roman Empire, this time a more spiritual one in which the pope, intermittently, served as the religious leader.

William's conquering of England meant Norman-style Christianity was on the move, replacing the Saxon style. Meanwhile, ordinary folk everywhere clung, as best they could, to their old pagan ways, even incorporating them into Christian plays so they would not be forgotten. The trick was to disguise such moments in theatrics so they might look Christian or harmless to priests and monks.

Ross understood that there were once gods for every season. Saints replaced them for most seasons, and then there were the memorable moments in the life of Jesus to cover the other bases. Halloween was originally a pagan celebration, but it gained Christian approval. It came during a northern hemisphere winter. It was a time when Europeans needed cheering up with the promise that winter wouldn't last forever; it would end, and there would be new growth. Christmas, the celebration of Jesus' birth, also serves as a means to bring joy and cheer to people.

Then there was Easter, with Jesus rising from the dead and the land in Europe coming good and green once more. The pagan elements related to renewal were prominent in this context. There was the egg and the rabbit. Young women dancing around the Maypole were also pagan; for centuries, no one seemed to mind. Ross hoped some stupid, politically correct fellow or a Woke idiot wouldn't raise future objections.

The legend of the Green Man harked back to a time of human sacrifice for some, though not others. Right up to the 20th Century, there was harmless fun in which men and, in some cases, women dressed in green to welcome the spring.

Ross read that those witches in Europe and England began as wise women and wise men. Traditions in healthcare handed down during pre-Christian times were attacked during the medieval period and later. Some cures were nonsense, while others contained some truth. The Church wanted complete control over what passed for medicine to maintain a firm hold on the peasantry. Only the Church had the authority to heal the sick. It was because of this need that the Church, and Christians in general, had to deal harshly with so-called witchcraft. This resulted in numerous executions in England during the English Civil War between the Cavaliers and the Roundheads (1642-1651).

By the 19th Century, Ross gathered that European science had made good progress in replacing superstition. The belief that witches could do actual harm or would even care to do so was put to rest.

In Australia, as far as Ross knew, the killing of witches hadn't caught on. It was in the USA, but only for a short period.

One of the USA's founding fathers, Benjamin Franklin, was a man of science, not superstition. He saw the value of capitalism and letting religions flourish unhindered, so long as no one got hurt. He had a printing press and viewed nature not as evil but as something to be studied.

Ross didn't care if the giving of Christmas presents had something to do with a Roman or Greek god. He didn't give a damn that it was Queen Victoria's husband that had made Christmas trees popular, first in England and then throughout the British Empire, including Australia. He understood why evergreens were so crucial in frigid countries in December. It was a way of remembering that ice and snow will eventually be replaced by green, not just evergreen.

It is true that Ross grew up with the heavier, northern meals at Christmas and that they had been replaced mainly by seafood in his old age. It came down to an understanding that in the northern hemisphere, during that time of year, there was the need to battle the cold with food, whereas in Australia, it was often swelteringly hot, and if a battle were to be waged, it would be with the heat.

Some people insisted on Happy Holidays replacing everything else. Ross insisted on saying Merry Christmas at Christmas time throughout his life, especially to the 'happy holidays' folk. He thought Happy Holidays kowtowed too much to first political correctness and then the Woke. He felt it was okay to say Happy Hanukkah to anyone Jewish to acknowledge their holiday.

Glenda understood he enjoyed giving the politically correct and the Woke heaps of abuse on social media. She wasn't sure why, so she asked him one day. He said: "They are the old witch hunters, communists and religious nutters only by a different name. They, therefore, deserve everything I can dish out to them and more."

"Would you be just as brave if you had to face them?" she asked.

"I did that as a public servant," he replied. "I could have gone further if I had kept my mouth shut, but couldn't simply stand by while certain injustices were happening."

"The Japanese woman attacking those Chinese workers?" she asked, touching her silvery hair with her hand.

"Yes," he replied. "I should have spoken up sooner, but didn't have the courage."

"You were brave in doing so," she told him with a smile. "Eventually, standing up, I mean."

"Yes," he said. "I like to think so. But I should have done so sooner!"

"Would it have made a difference?" she asked.

"Apart from making me feel better?" he replied. "No difference at all."

CHAPTER ELEVEN

You Only Want One Thing

The system was all about killing passion and love. What Ross Martin wanted most in his teens and early twenties, he got with Glenda Evens in those two good years near the end of his life. Even though it was mainly cuddling with a bit of sex thrown in, it was still appreciated. It had come decades too late to impact his overall life—no decades-old memories for Ross.

Still, Ross and Glenda enjoyed each other as best they could with the time they had together, and that was something. It could have been worse. His life could have ended with nothing but regrets.

Taking up ballroom dancing in old age was beneficial. He had always liked Jazz and the big band sound. His sister had talked him into it, and dancing with Glenda had been the start of their lives together. He had danced with other women, but with Glenda the most. It was probably no surprise to her when he asked if she wanted to get coffee with him one night after the dance. She smiled, and miraculously, everything he wanted to fall into place did so. He was honest and straightforward with Glenda, which made all the difference.

Jem, who bit him when they were young, once told him he only wanted one thing from girls. She didn't elaborate, but she was right. But not from her because he thought she was ugly, but he did desire it from others. There were pretty girls in primary and high school.

First, the kiss, and to see where that might lead. In her teasing, Jem convinced him that he should pretend not to want it so much and go for other things. He didn't know what these non-sex-related things might be, and he found it challenging to envision peddling snake oil when he had no idea what snake oil would be best to peddle or how it should be presented.

He came away from Jem, thinking he needed to be a secret agent or a damn good salesman. After high school, he turned out to be neither. He didn't know what to say as a secret agent, and as a salesman, the snake oil he came up with was unpopular.

There were kids at his high school with car magazines and Playboys. He would have liked to have become better acquainted with car parts, but that only happened when he got a car. It was like the kids with the car magazines spoke a foreign language. Did they even understand what they were talking about?

His first auto was a second-hand Morris 1500. It served him well for a couple of years. It wasn't the fastest of cars, but it could get him from Sydney to the Gold Coast without breaking down. Then he replaced it with a Toyota Corolla. It was not a good buy. A gasket kept blowing and had to be replaced repeatedly, and no matter what mechanics tried, the brakes remained spongy.

Playboys were fine for a first look at the naked female form, but that was about it. The type of photography used always made the women look surreal. Lines were smoothed over, and desirable features were enhanced. *Anyone who doesn't believe the camera can tell porkies should check out these nudie mags,* thought Ross one day.

He noticed that fashion magazine covers were being manipulated. There was once a model well known for her freckles, but in one issue of one of those magazines, her freckles went walkabout. A magazine editor didn't like freckles.

When he was past thirty and in college, he went on a few dates, but nothing came of them.

He drank over college weekends, which didn't help at all. He was told he wasn't to think about the women he wanted to be close to as objects. That seemed fair enough, but how should he feel about them? What did they want? And what should he be thinking when he came upon women who treated men as sex objects? He had never wolf-whistled in his life, and he couldn't imagine women whistling at him.

When a good-looking blonde woman treated him as less than human at a college party, he knew he didn't want to have anything to do with her. She was too much the ice goddess, and he knew he could not melt her frozen heart. She had a boyfriend anyway. He was into football, and they were part of the football elite. Ross was the outsider.

He couldn't be friends with her or them. He imagined she and the football star she was so fond of were forever wearing these invisible crowns that propelled their noses to rise well above their mouths to escape the foul smell of the peasantry. Both had vassals. He imagined them having this fantastic sex life. Was he wrong? He was right, but this didn't make them human. They were the closest thing to aristocracy or perhaps androids he was ever likely to meet. Did they think beyond their stations in life? He didn't believe they did. Why should they anyway when all they could want was laid at their feet?

Ross, through them and their attitudes toward him, could understand why some down-and-outs in the USA took up guns to execute football stars and their minions.

He went to the theatre at college, hoping it might do something for him. Some of the young women in the acting class wanted to be his friend, but that was it. At least, that was something. He went to dinner with one of them, but nothing came of that. However, it was his first time on the back of a motorbike, so it wasn't a complete waste.

He discovered that he enjoyed writing for the theatre, but he had much to learn. For example, he had to pick a setting that would sing to an audience and develop characters that viewers could identify. Also, he had to work around the limitations of the stage. For example, having a hundred actors walking on and off would be too costly for most theatre company productions, especially for a new and, therefore, untried play. A handful of performers, then, would be better. As an actor, he knew he would never be a leading man, which was all right with him. He could even tolerate a footballer being the lead. He thought he might make it as a comedian. He could do a sad sack.

Unfortunately, the college didn't encourage the writing and development of new plays. They couldn't risk not getting enough bums on seats. He got a play about Vietnam staged there, but knew it wasn't a great success. He hadn't done enough research. There would, however, be such successes in his future where there was nothing wrong with his grasp of the subject matter. He would come to realise over time that patrons were happier with comedies from new playwrights rather than dramas. Make them laugh, and then see what can be done in other areas of theatrical writing.

Immediately after college, he tried a local theatre group. There, he could learn more about acting but not writing for the theatre. Those involved in theatrical productions were not interested in seeing new scripts. A decade later, that would change. In the meantime, he learned more about short plays and how they were put together.

He had seen some marvellous theatre enacted at college and then on stage locally at Cronulla. There was one actress at college he thought had much strength in her acting (she once played Major Barbara in a college production), but when it came to television, she was given such wimpy roles that it wasn't a wonder she never became a star. Some fool must have thought making her teary-eyed much of the time would be suitable for her career when the opposite was true. Ross could praise her acting in college productions, but could hardly stomach what they got her to do on television.

After college, he had a short affair with an older woman that lasted a month. She was pretty with a dazzling smile. Then she went back to France, and that was that. He wasn't surprised his writer and artist friends didn't believe it had happened. Making love to a French woman was such a cliché. She was the woman he might have invented. She had a round face, hazel eyes, curly short hair and purred when satisfied. She was petite and knew how to dress well.

She was in bed with him numerous times, and he wondered why. He got the one thing plus for a short while from her and was so happy that he had done so. He had no idea how long it would last or, when it was over, how long the memories of it would have to sustain him, keeping dark thoughts at bay.

Ross wondered if women ever wanted just one thing from guys. He suspected it was the case with that French woman.

Commercials in the 1990s suggested a woman's appetite for more than just one thing, plus. The men in those ads, specifically created for women, were the sporty type. That wasn't him, but then again, there were lots of women around he wouldn't classify as the sporty type, either. There were all sorts of women out there in the wide world of the 1990s and beyond, and he was always hopeful that one of them he found attractive would feel the same way about him, too. He didn't want someone grotesque, but, at the same time, knew he didn't need someone so outside his class (he was a 7 out of 10) that it couldn't last past a one-night stand.

He recalled, smilingly, when the movie 10, starring Dudley Moore, Julie Andrews, and Bo Derek, first came out. It was near the beginning of the 1980s. Then, a decade later, he and other office men played the one-to-ten rating game regarding the office women.

CHAPTER TWELVE

Is Disco That Bad?

The lack of a good connection between music and Ross Martin was part of the system formed against him. Because he wasn't very good at Maths in primary school, he was not allowed to learn how to read music and play a musical instrument. The same was true for high school. He didn't think to ask any of the teachers why this was so, nor did his parents.

Not being permitted to learn and play stuck with him, even after he left high school and was old enough to make his own choices. He suspected that learning about music early on might have helped him with Math, but the system decided this would not be the case. Thus, he was profoundly isolated from that world of sound.

Even so, he enjoyed the singing of the Andrews Sisters in movies starring Bud Abbott and Lou Costello made during World War II. His favourite Andrews Sisters song was "Drinking Rum and Coca-Cola." Years later, he would drink scotch and Coke to avoid getting too bored at discos.

He liked the road movies of Bing Crosby and Bob Hope, his favourite being the Road to Bali. Bing Crosby played the conman in them, and Bob Hope played the fall guy. There was singing, lots of humour, and nothing to be taken seriously.

He liked the introduction tune to *The Lone Ranger* television show. He only got the cane when he argued with a primary school teacher, saying the William Tell Overture was that tune. The makers, first of the radio program and then the television series *The Lone Ranger*, had taken a portion of the William Tell Overture and made it their own. In this, cane or no cane, young Ross was right. The cane was an injustice, but one he could live with because, for an instant, he was a bad boy.

Later, Ross was to discover that the opening tune to *The Green Hornet* movie serials and television show was derived from *Flight of the Bumblebee*. Thus was Ross's strange introduction to classical music. He tried at one stage to take classical music seriously, but it wasn't for him. Much of it was too slow and complicated, and he preferred music with good visuals.

He recalled listening to *Peter and the Wolf* in primary school. In this piece of music, each character in the unfolding story is represented by a musical instrument. Like the rest of the class, he found it all a yawn. Even when Disney threw in animation and put the results on television, it didn't help much.

His dad enjoyed Westerns and the music that accompanied them. The opening song to the television show *Rawhide* was a favourite. In the 1960s, numerous Westerns were featured on television. They included *Rifleman, Lawman, Annie Oakley, Gunsmoke, Bat Masterson,* and *Broken Arrow.*

From his study of American history, Ross realised that most of these shows were glamorised versions of the lives of famous people. The exception was *Gunsmoke*, which took a more realistic approach to the Western genre.

There were also episodes of *Rawhide* he felt didn't stray too far from the way it was during those big 19th-century cattle drives. One such episode he thought of as highly fictitious until a New Zealand farmer put him straight. In the episode, static electricity caused the horns of the cattle to glow in the dark at night and spook them. She told him this could happen since the hollow horns could glow.

In the television series *Annie Oakley*, starring Gail Davis, she was made out to be part of the law in a fictional town. They did get her height right (she wasn't very tall), and she did have an extraordinary ability with a rifle, as demonstrated in the show.

Both his parents were fond of Country singers such as Slim Dusty. His mother liked American singer Nat King Cole, who once had his own television show. She particularly liked the song "Mona Lisa."

Reaching his teens, Ross thought something in Jazz and Blues might be worth exploring. Then, anti-war songs such as Billy Don't Be a Hero caught his attention and imagination. The war in Vietnam dragged on with no end in sight, and the question of whether Australian troops should be there at all was on the minds of many Australians.

M*A*S*H, the television show, was based on the Korean War and started as a comedy, but ultimately, it was about the futility of war. Back then, in the 1970s, Ross understood that Americans couldn't have a show that was too negative about what was happening in Vietnam. The theme song, "Suicide is Painless," was a real grabber. It left Ross questioning himself, his place in the world, and whether continuing was worthwhile.

In old age, Ross Martin's partner was the music guru of the household. Glenda loved to listen to jazz while cooking or cleaning. He preferred the television in the next room when engaged in either task. He liked music accompanied by dialogue and the impression that people were interacting with one another. It stemmed from decades of living alone, with nothing but the television for company. He liked the radio whenever they travelled, but only on those occasions. He found the knowledge that there were faces on a screen comforting. He didn't think this was normal, but he no longer cared.

Ross recalled the first record he ever purchased: Snoopy versus the Red Baron by the Red Guardsmen. Years later, he saw the Red Guardsmen perform the song on YouTube.

He was a Peanuts fan and often thought his luck ran the way it did for Charlie Brown. Looking in the mirror, Ross saw himself as the round-headed kid. His sister, Kate, was sometimes like Lucy. He remembered one Saturday chasing her around the table for getting him up too early, then the reverse, after she got mad, and she chased him. Not many years later, they became great friends and remained so. He found she was always on his side, whether she agreed or disagreed with him.

Ross, at first, understood why his mother and father were against long hair on guys. Both had grown up in an era when short hair on men was the norm. Once *The Beatles* became popular, and long hair was viewed as a protest against the Vietnam War, they both changed their minds. *Jesus Christ Superstar* came along, which also helped promote long hair. He remembered the local Methodist preacher not favouring this, and a sign outside the church that read, "Jesus is Not a Superstar!"

A drive Ross took with his sister, Kate, was forever memorable. They went from New South Wales into Queensland in a Morris 1500 he owned. They listened to *Beatles* music most of the way. There were adventurous moments. They went through a storm of yellow butterflies, a bull chased their car, and they came upon a giant snake.

Ross parked the car to get a better look at the snake and take a photograph of it. It appeared to be asleep. He took photos from all angles. It woke up when he was on the wrong side of it. While it was still groggy, he walked around it and returned to his Morris. Behind the wheel, he could have started the engine and run over the snake. Instead, he waited for it to slither away. On another occasion, his father wanted to run over a similar snake, but Ross wouldn't let him. Maybe his father thought he was squeamish about killing the snake, but that wasn't the case. To live and let live with snakes seemed to him to be the best policy. They ate vermin, which he preferred not to deal with when fishing, so they were an asset.

Years later, he was working at Wellington in New South Wales when he saw an Aborigine boy about to chuck a rock at a bird. He told the boy that if he killed it, he should eat it. This confused the boy and he didn't chuck the rock. Word of what he said got around, and the Aboriginal elders saw him in a better light. He had inadvertently said what they considered to be the right thing. That also stayed with him. His dad had taught him to throw a fish he had caught back into the water that he didn't intend to cook and eat.

Ross thought he might get somewhere with the opposite sex if he went to discos. Maybe if he had just gone there for the music and the dancing, he wouldn't have been so disappointed with the experience. He thought discos would be the child of making love, not war. They turned out to be places where you could listen to soppy disco music, Rock 'n Roll, and whatever else was around, dance, drink, and nothing else.

He became jaded by the simple setting and the large ball with the reflective glass rectangles, which belonged to the 1920s, so he kept drinking. Most of these discos were converted warehouses, where those who ran them realised the money was in having a bar and a large dance floor with enough chairs and tables for people to rest. He soon realised that the young women dancing were the same ones he had seen on television on channel two, so it was no big deal. His dancing with them was the only reason to be there besides the grog.

Some venues hired live bands that were so bad, they were lucky to last six months before fading away for good. He got the occasional dance with a lovely, but nothing more than a dance came his way. He had to admit that he didn't know what to expect or do other than silly movements on the dance floor with someone he didn't know. He winged it that way for a handful of Friday nights, something he was never good at, then concluded that whatever was going on he didn't know about, he would never find out about anyway.

He was not *The Saint*. He was far from suave, sophisticated, and good-looking.

Ross would leave the disco and go home drunk on the train. He would wish he had not consumed so much Dutch courage, which only served to empty his wallet. The next day would be a blur to him.

He couldn't imagine a future with a woman. He would later understand it as the most insidious part of the system he wanted to defeat. If he couldn't see himself with that woman and that better life, what chance did he have of success?

At college, he attended a country-style dance where country music was played. It was fun, but it was a one-off.

A college friend, Penelope, once took Ross to a ballet performance in Sydney. He recalled it was Swan Lake. For him, it wasn't all that exciting. He wasn't a leg man, but he could appreciate the skill that went into such events. One of the female dancers had her top slip, revealing her tiny breasts. She kept on dancing. He thought he was the only one who had noticed and mentioned it to Penelope. This may be why she never invited him to the ballet again. *I am a barbarian*, thought Ross with a smile after telling her.

Penelope had him join her at a pub in the inner city of Sydney one night to listen to a new band doing their thing. Being there with nothing to watch except musicians playing bored him. He tried not to reveal this to Penelope, but he must have sighed one time too much, so she got the hint. He went with her to see *Midnight Oil* at a better venue, and again, he needed to be more thoroughly entertained.

However, seeing *The Divinyls* live with her in Surry Hills was beautiful. It was deep into summer, and the place was overcrowded.

They were both sweating like crazy, but it was okay. They, and the rest of the people there, were excited, and that band possibly never gave a better performance in their lives. The singer, Chrissy Amphlett, splashed the audience with cold water between songs. This Ross had never seen a singer do before or since.

Later in life, he saw stage musical performances in Sutherland; sometimes, this was with Penelope, and at other times, with his sister, Kate. In the earlier years of knowing Penelope, she sometimes had on this lipstick that made her breath smell of fresh strawberries. In the Spring, she wore a vanilla fragrance that he felt suited that time of year, as spring is a time of renewal and hope. He was always fascinated by how Penelope wrinkled up her nose when she smiled or how she would absentmindedly play with her long blond hair, even when it went from blond to silver.

Did he love her? He sometimes thought he did, but didn't have the right to do so. He was not like his brother, Ian. He was never stocky. He was either thin or fat. He was not the kind of chancer she adored as a sexual partner. She would eventually be divorced from such a person. He overthought before acting and, in doing so, remained single. Also, she loved motorbikes, and he had never owned one. *Easy Rider* was her favourite movie.

One play he especially liked was *The Producers*. It was about two chancers working off the notion that they could make more money with a poorly made play than a well-made one. Another was *Young Frankenstein*. He saw both with Penelope.

Ross missed out on seeing a play he wanted to see, but in missing out, he discovered he could be part of the world of live theatre. Being able to write for actors gave him a great sense of well-being and improved his life. He was still the odd man out, but among some other weird people, it often didn't matter. He wasn't much good with names, and that was to play havoc with him, but that couldn't be helped.

He recalled train trips where someone would play American ghetto music. He would look around as the train came into various stations and noted that he was not living in a slum, and so ghetto music was nothing but an irritant. The south coast of New South Wales had its beauty spots, and no one was getting mowed down by thugs with machine guns wearing bandanas.

Ross took up ballroom dancing in old age, which is how he met Glenda. Previously, he recalled learning the moves in high school. There was a day when his dance partner, a girl he had never considered pretty, was sick, so he came to dance with the girl's physical education teacher. She smelled nice, and dancing close to her was such a pleasure.

This was what he would have liked to have been a part of the Disco experience, but that was not to be. Was it Disco's fault? No. It was just how the times were when he was a young man. He figured the hippies had won; the Vietnam War came to an end for Australians in 1972. After that, those hippies didn't know what to do with themselves since making love, not war, had lost much of its meaning. They were to go back to the old ways of being. They would marry, raise children, and generally live what most of us would call respectable lives.

It was in the mid-1970s that Ross had entered his first Disco. Long hair was still in fashion, but that was it. No one who didn't want to go was being forced to enter military service. Ross learned from a friend that those who did could learn skills without paying for the privilege. Skills that could see them right for the rest of their lives, like how to cook like a chef, handle radio equipment or repair a jeep or truck. Also, it was a place to learn self-discipline and respect for others.

In the 1960s and 1970s, civilian men living in Western-style countries were not supposed to cook. This fact was paraded on television. The movie *To Sir with Love*, however, raised the question of what a bloke fresh out of school living alone could do to feed himself rather than continually relying on takeout. It was a question of simple but filling meals that were affordable.

Ross, living independently, found he had to learn how to cook at least simple meals. He recalled sharing a house with a terrible woman and her kid. Having loaned her money to cover the rent, he only had cash for baked beans. He had a decent job, yet he couldn't provide himself with a good meal for a few days. And yes, he felt hard done by.

In the early 21st Century, there was much television to do with music Ross didn't like. There were also cooking shows galore on TV. The only one he cared for was one in which an attractive English woman was doing the cooking. She had a charm and an elegance about her that he found captivating. She spoke with a plum in her mouth, but it wasn't forced. It was just her natural way of talking.

There was *Australia's Got Talent* and *The Voice*. The only saving grace for *The Voice* was that Ross's sister loved the show. Why she loved it would remain a mystery to him. Penelope also thought it wasn't lousy viewing. She told him it gave people a chance to shine, which wasn't bad. "You can be an old grump," she told him one night, "but that's okay. I like you anyway."

In old age, Ross still winced at the sound of *Disco Duck* and other mind-numbing Disco numbers. He was glad he never landed in a nursing home where the residents were expected to exercise to the sound of the Bee Gees *Staying Alive!* His answer, in zombie fashion, to anyone in that imagined nursing home would be: "I'd rather not, thank you very much."

Why Clothes Don't Always Make the Man

The system never wanted Ross Martin to do well. Occasionally, something got in his way that wasn't the system's doing but was something the system could use. It had much to do with how he thought of himself and presented himself to others.

Ross had never been much good at picking out clothes for himself. If he had been better at it, he might have beaten the system sooner rather than later. There was that ghastly purple suit he had his mother buy him for his 21st birthday. Maybe it would have been okay for the fictional DC character the Joker to wear, but not a young man, such as himself, unless he was going to a costume party. Later, there was a safari suit that would have suited Jungle Jim but not him. By the time he entered college, he had given up on a suit that would impress anyone.

He knew of guys who dressed nicely and did all right with women. He envied them but couldn't see his way clear to being one of them. He never felt relaxed in a suit, even a good one. It was as if he were pretending to be someone else and not getting away with it.

Ross had a handful of ties in his drawer that he rarely wore. One represented the college from which he had graduated. All the others were cheap and looked that way, too. After a while, he forgot how to tie a tie, but that was only a problem for him at weddings and funerals.

He understood bright colours could be a problem, giving off signals he preferred not to give off. Pink was for surfers and gays, not Ross. There were other traps. He once bought short pants that had multiple pockets. His sister, Kate, thought they were a bit la-de-da, so he didn't get much use out of them and, for a while, gave short pants a miss. *You can't go wrong with jeans*, he thought. Years later, Kate persuaded him to wear short pants to get sun on his legs in the summer. He was vitamin D deficient, so she thought that might help.

One Christmas, Penelope gave him this black thing with holes, which might have been a T-shirt or a black singlet. He imagined going to the beach in it and ending up with unusual sunburns. He couldn't see himself wearing it in public, so it remained in a drawer for a few years before it ended up with the Salvation Army. He, of course, thanked her for the gift, though he had no idea why she thought it would suit him.

One day, while on a train heading to a railway job, Ross noticed a police officer politely asking a young man to produce a railway ticket. This fellow became flustered and agitated when he couldn't do it immediately. He was wearing long pants with a dozen pockets. He went through them until, with an air of triumph, he showed the ticket to the policeman. Ross was amazed at how this officer remained calm throughout all this.

Ross tended to buy cheap shoes that fell apart after six months' worth of wear. This was especially true when he was working for the railways. It was close to the end of his life, and he wore sensible and a tad more expensive footwear at the insistence of his sister and his lady love, Glenda. He and his sister attributed his fall and broken arm to wearing poorly made shoes.

Ross remembered the time he was cleaning out this attic for the newspaper he was working for. He was told to wear clothes he didn't mind getting dirty in. He was given a dust coat, but some of the dust still got on his clothing. He went to a post office at lunchtime to mail a few letters. There, he had to cue up. Behind him, he heard this woman complaining about dole bludgers mailing letters at that time of day, on her lunch hour, when they were free to do so any other time of the day. He knew she was talking about him. He was about to correct her when he reached the person behind the counter, who gave him the stamps and sent him on his way.

Years later, when working for the railways, he was on his way to an afternoon job that would end late at night at a station when he overheard a woman talking about how Australian men would instead not be employed but ride the rails like hobos. He knew she was chatting to her companion about him, but didn't care. He thought the notion of him being a hobo amusing.

The people Ross worked with on the trains and buses tended to dress down rather than up. The drinking of alcohol while working was forbidden, as was the taking of drugs. A couple of the people he worked with were tested and came up clean. He didn't mind being tested, but that never happened. There were pubs he went to for a meal or simply a coffee, but never anything intoxicating. He liked the work and wanted to keep on doing it. At Berry, a pub served a reasonably priced thick, juicy country-style steak.

One cold morning, Ross went to a pub for coffee. The bartender asked him to remove his hood, which was keeping his ears warm. He did so and, in complying, realised the overhead camera would have trouble recognising him with the hood on. He hadn't thought of that when he entered. Did the hood part of his jacket make him a suspicious character? He thought that might be the case.

He was always trying to figure out how to dress for the changing seasons, from winter to spring and summer to autumn. If he put on a jumper and it turned out to be a hot day, he would have to carry it in his backpack. He'd freeze if he didn't bring a jumper and it turned out cold. He generally sided with caution and brought along a jumper.

Growing up in the 1960s and 1970s, Ross was unsure about hats. No one young wore them. Fewer older men had them. Long hair prevents getting too sunburned on top by the sun in summer. Then, sometime in the 1980s, a trend emerged for wearing caps incorrectly. He thought that was silly and not for him.

In the 1990s, he considered wearing an Akubra hat, but a fellow he didn't like, who was connected to the music industry, started wearing one, which meant an Akubra was out for him. He sighed profoundly, thinking it was a damned shame. He cursed that bastard of a music twit and left it at that. Besides, Akubras were expensive, and he didn't want to pay for anything that would make him look bad because of someone he didn't like.

His hair was thinning, and a hat would have helped keep sunburn away in summer. He thought an Akubra would have given him a rugged look until that fellow took that possibility away. Eventually, Glenda found him a hat that was not associated with anyone or anything he could disapprove of, and that was that. She discovered it, among others, at Kangaroo Valley.

Ross always felt Glenda dressed well, even going to the corner store for bread and milk. Gone were the days when women past middle age dyed their hair blue to cover up their greying hair. Ross had yet to learn why it was ever done. Maybe it was just a 1970s fashion in Australia. He could say he dressed neatly and cleanly for Glenda, but that was it. Books and DVDS meant more to him than clothes because, unlike clothes, they had never let him down.

CHAPTER FOURTEEN

Alphabet Soup!

Ross Martin grew up when there were only males and females, and nothing else. Men were supposed to be interested in women, and women were supposed to be interested in men. There was talk of pansies, but he always thought this had to do with being weak and nothing more. He didn't want ever to appear to be weak.

In the 1960s, nothing other than male-female relations was depicted on television. He understood that in high school, he would have an uphill battle getting to know the opposite sex physically. This he accepted.

What he found monstrous in the 1970s was the notion that some men didn't want to have anything physically to do with women, and some women didn't want anything physically to do with men. It came as a shock because, up until then, it had been a secret that no one in the media had discussed.

The Australian soap *Number 96* had two gay characters, and at least one gay guy in *The Box*, another Australian soap of the day. In *Number 96*, gays were supposed to be intellectuals. Maybe some gays in real life were like that, but the gays in *Number 96* didn't always get their movie facts right. With *The Box*, there was a shower scene. It was in its first episode that the people of Melbourne could appreciate it, but it was censored for the people of New South Wales. It was thus that Ross missed out on seeing on television a young woman in the nude.

Ross's aunt had a strange brother. Surprisingly, Ross never knew until the 1970s. This brother of his aunt, however, would play a critical role in misunderstandings between him and his aunt, resulting in some years of him seething with hatred toward gays. Of course, the gays were not even remotely responsible. No. It was his daffy aunt. When he worked that out, his hatred toward gays lessened and then eventually ceased. Why hate people who didn't want to do him harm, who just wanted to live their own lives their way?

He didn't want to be sidelined because of others' peculiar passions. He didn't want sympathy from some woman who would then cut him off at the knees for the sake of people he didn't care about one way or the other and didn't want to care about. Ultimately, he saw them as fellow human beings with a different outlook on life, but was not thankful that his loopy aunt was turning either him or them into villains. He didn't have to be what she thought he was, and he didn't have to attack anyone with a different lifestyle.

Ross understood how some came to see guys who hadn't dated many women. You are a write-off if they think you are not trying hard enough or don't eat rusty nails for breakfast, downed with gasoline, and topped off with a lit cigar. He hated the very idea of being written off.

He attended weight training in high school, but that didn't work. He was then placed in a judo class, but the instructor reassigned him to a weight training class. By this time, he had had enough of high school fitness. He avoided sports during his last six months of high school and spent that time studying for his final exams. He felt the people who were supposed to make him fit had failed miserably.

In college, some women came up with the idea that gay men were a boon to heterosexual men. They claimed that the more gays there were around, the more opportunities for heterosexuals. Ross knew this to be false.

If there was a village of forty men and half were gay, and there were also forty women who were all heterosexual, then you might think twenty male heterosexuals would be privileged, thought Ross one night. But what if those women, instead of seeing twenty gay guys, saw twenty-one instead? To what advantage, then, were the twenty gay guys to that one heterosexual male the women think is gay? Answer: no advantage at all.

Ross was a good runner and enjoyed fishing and bushwalking. Eventually, wildlife photography became his passion. When he worked in the country once, he tried Twilight Bowls and found them enjoyable.

One time, playing games of French cricket with factory workers was fine, but it didn't make up for the fact that he didn't care to watch cricket on TV. He didn't understand why waiting for a batter to whack a hard ball was so masculine. On the other hand, pounding the ball was probably masculine unless done by a young woman. By the time the 20th Century closed, there were women's soccer and cricket teams.

Living in a sporting nation meant being wrapped up in some sport or being an outsider. He didn't see the importance of running up and down a field chasing a ball. Perhaps his lack of interest began in Primary School before he received his first pair of glasses. Maybe he didn't see well enough to get into soccer or rugby at an early age.

He knew that neither fishing nor bushwalking cut it in the society he was living in. Unless you fished on the rocks, there was little danger in fishing and virtually none in bushwalking unless you came upon a snake. Danger seemed to be the answer. The more dangerous the activity, the more women adored the male players. He was glad Glenda wasn't like that unless she thought wildlife photography deadly.

During his two years with Glenda, the Alphabet People, sponsored by the Woke, came into being. Neither he nor his lady love understood what they were talking about. What he could make out was that some were gay, wanting to have the body parts of the other. Thanks to science, this was possible. He was against kids altering their bodies in such a way because he felt that such decisions should be left until they were adults and better understood what they were willing to do to themselves, especially since such changes were often impossible or nearly impossible to reverse. Glenda concurred.

Then, some wanted to change the English language by replacing "him" and "her" with "them" instead. He wasn't sure how many sexes the Woke thought there were. He considered it in the hundreds and wondered how an office building could have enough bathrooms for hundreds of people of so many sexes to cope. He thought about cyborgs. Would they need unique bathrooms for grease and oil changes?

He was so glad he wasn't a kid in the early 21st Century, wondering what to do about the army of different sexes that had materialised seemingly overnight. He felt the attacks upon the Harry Potter novels and their author by the Alphabet People were unwarranted. He was happy with his collection of those books.

"We're good together," he told Glenda after a walk along the nearby beach. "All the nut cases in all the world can't take that away from us."

"They might try," Glenda told him, "But they have no chance of success."

"The Alphabet people and their soup are for others," he told her. "Not for me."

CHAPTER FIFTEEN

Why Sport Doesn't Make the Cut

Was finding a sport and mastering it a way of breaking the back of the system? Ross Martin considered this a possibility, but it had to be a contact sport. Nothing else would do it. He knew this from primary onward, but it wasn't for him, and anything else didn't have the right impact.

Just before Ross met Glenda, his nephew used his brain to be good at soccer and thus live a more sociable life. Ross had no idea that could be done until his sister Kate's offspring did it.

Ross once read somewhere that humans are an aggressive species, and sport is needed to stop them from killing each other on a more regular basis. He thought there was something in that.

Team sports were supposed to create camaraderie, but that never happened to him. Sport didn't become the glue of his life the way it had for others. For the best boss he ever had in that government office, it was vital and the basis for putting together a great office team. It was through this fellow that Ross could gather how rugby could improve one's life if given a chance to do so.

He recalled cricket and how it might have helped him. His dad had played it in his youth, and he had cousins keen on the game. If he had gone in for it, his life could have changed for the better, but that did not happen. He found nothing duller than watching cricket on television. He recalled a match around December one year in which the announcer got so bored that he began talking about what the seagulls were doing on the green.

He was fine watching tennis, but that wasn't a team sport. And none of this played well with his cousins. There was something masculine about cricket and football that they could understand, but he could not. He imagined punching the crap out of one of them if that would do any good. Upon reflection, it might have achieved something. Were they into boxing? He didn't think so, but there was that possibility.

His dad showed him the game of golf, but that didn't take. He enjoyed whacking away at golf balls with a club but never pressed his old man to teach him the game. In his later years, he wished he had done so.

Ross recalled playing softball in primary school as part of PE. Forty boys and girls were all indifferent to the game. Ross and the others got to do fielding, but had to wait their turn at bat. Often, for most of them, that turn never came. Time ran out. The result? Ross and most other kids waiting sat on the green and dug for the roots of onion grass, the only exercise they were likely to get as batters. Ross learned that having too many kids for some sports spoils enthusiasm. He also liked the taste of onion grass bulbs. They tasted like celery, only with a bit of dirt added. Was there still onion grass in the world? Fifty years later, in another part of New South Wales, with the woman he loved, he had to wonder about that.

While working as a salesman in Sydney, he took up tennis before college. He thought a young player might be interested in him. Her boyfriend told him she was already taken, which was okay with him.

He would have preferred it if she had said so, but the guy was friendly enough with the information, and Ross didn't mind that. Tennis was good exercise and fun.

Penelope was at college with him but was keener on another fencer, so fencing didn't work out, but he enjoyed playing Zorro anyway.

Years earlier, when he had a stint in the library section of a newspaper (also known as the morgue because that was where dead stories ended up), he learned that it was gay guys who were the fellows who took the page two girlie pics. The story going around was that a straight fellow taking pics of half-naked models day in and day out would go nuts if he didn't get enough action from them.

After college, Ross imagined seeing all these Penelopes, in their underwear or swimsuits, parading before him day in and day out, and him going crazy over no physical contact. Hence, he figured the gossipmongers at that newspaper got it right back then.

He remembered an ad on television when he worked for that newspaper. In it, there was an Asian guy who dabs on this aftershave and then gets mobbed by thousands of half-dressed women. Another ad, made decades later for aftershave, featured a man sprinkling it on himself. He dies of a heart attack brought on by all the attention from all these beautiful women. It doesn't end there, for a worm exits his grave and ends up at the bottom of a bottle of tequila. Some fellow drinks the tequila, eats the worm and is suddenly adored by all these women.

An ad that got banned by some spoilsports was for Ant's Pants. It showed ants climbing up an attractive young woman's bare legs, and she called for Rex to sort them out. Rex is a spiny anteater who grumbles but is obedient.

Ross wondered what his cousins would have thought of hockey as a sport if he had played hockey. They probably would have considered it a lame excuse for soccer. Ah! However, if ice hockey is played in the

USA or Canada, and there is plenty of blood on the ice, they may have a different opinion. The blood would have been the key! A split lip, a black eye, or a broken nose! Ha! He would have become one of them, for sure, after that!

After college, Ross met Penelope for movie nights. They also played squash together. The squash game was enjoyable, but that was all.

Ross lost interest in photography in college but took it up again while working for the railroad. He found that every train station he was at presented him with something unique to photograph. Unanderra had the nearby Buddhist temple, Redfern had metal spears decorating the sidewalk, and Central had a train platform designed to take bodies to the cemetery.

He was enthusiastic about birding with a camera because it combined exercise with the creativity of getting the best shots of native wildlife. He roamed the south coast of New South Wales, looking for the unusual and sometimes finding it. He was thrilled when he came across his first black cockatoo. Then there was his first Silvereye and his first Dollar Bird.

When he visited New Zealand, it was as a writer and a birder with a camera. He stayed a few nights at a small township on the central north island with a writer friend who owned a farm. He was amazed at how many English birds had become wild in Australia and New Zealand during his travels there. They included sparrows and blackbirds. There was one bird Ross came across on a hill overlooking Auckland in New Zealand, but he has yet to find it in Australia, even though it had initially come from Europe. It was the yellowhammer, a little yellow bird.

Near the end of his life, Ross met Glenda Evens at a ballroom dance. This was something a team sport had never given him and never would. He wondered if his cousins would have been surprised by him with this second beautiful woman. He had forgiven them for the Penelope incident, and they had undoubtedly moved on with their lives.

Still, the hurt at being regarded as unworthy of being in the company of female beauty did linger for some time. Yet, he felt no form of attack appropriate. They had their opinion of him, and that was that.

Ross met his cousins at another family get-together decades after the Penelope incident, and they seemed to be better company. Old age was setting in, and the need for bloodletting was gone. There was no need to punch anyone in the nose anymore to prove some vague point or to be appreciated by his cousins.

CHAPTER SIXTEEN

Drinking, Smoking and Drugs

It was at college that Ross Martin came close to becoming an alcoholic. Being in a dorm with young people who couldn't understand why he wasn't more knowledgeable about social interactions got to him. He couldn't help but feel that the system was responsible for his lack of understanding of social cues. There were those years in which he was over twenty-one but looked younger.

He had to admit, if only to himself, that alcohol could make him dopey and often too sad to be of any use to anyone, including himself. There were happy drunks. At college, he just wasn't one of them. He remembered starting sociable enough with high expectations and the self-confident glow that alcohol can give one. It was then he would have been better off stopping, but he always had it in his mind to continue drinking to retain that glow. It was always a wrong decision because, after the glow, there was the inevitable decline.

After college, he only drank on Saturday nights when he was with artists. This was fine since, on those nights, he often quit drinking when still in a mellow mood. Drinking was expensive, and he would rather spend money on books and DVDS. With books and DVDS, he had something he could keep with him for a long time. Empty cans and bottles were different.

He fell into getting drunk every night when he shared a house with a woman and her teenage son. He couldn't use his computer in his room without the kid disturbing him. The laptop would make a start-up sound, the teen's cue to rap on his door. After a while, he gave up on using the computer and went to drink. He drank the cheapest forms of alcohol he could find and ate very little.

Having a unit of his own, he could live alone and freely. He drank only sociably, which meant sharing a bottle of wine on a Saturday with his artist friends and a few beers on Christmas and his birthday. At that rate, he wouldn't make anyone who owned a pub rich. After he met Glenda Evens and they moved in together, his drinking habits didn't change. There was no need for them to do so.

Ross was never keen on other people smoking, especially those puffing away on menthols or Turkish cigarettes. They got up his nose in the wrong way and made him cough. He remembered one time kissing a young woman who had been smoking. He didn't like the experience. He could smell tobacco on her, and her tongue burned his with tobacco juice. From then on, he would limit his kissing to women who didn't smoke.

His sister Kate tried smoking but quickly gave it up. He had a go with marijuana at college, but ended that when he left college. His brother, Ian, and his wife smoked. They also did drugs.

Ross couldn't fully understand why so many people smoked. It was such a filthy habit. One reason was that quitting was hard. Most, like his brother, Ian, started when they were kids. Also, smoking was prevalent in a lot of movies and television shows. It was why his dad had been hooked on them for decades, and it had been such a struggle for him to give them up.

Western novels and films often had men either smoking or chewing tobacco. In silent movies, like the ones he saw in college, female rebels smoked and drank. Ross recalled one of the stars of the 1990s show *Sex in the City* smoking cigars.

He remembered when cigarette advertisements were banned at sporting events. Then, each cigarette packet came with photographic evidence of what could happen to a smoker who kept on smoking. Smoking was then forbidden in offices, pubs and restaurants. The question of why public hospitals should admit patients who are sick from smoking was raised. Shouldn't they instead have to go to private hospitals since their ailments had been self-inflicted?

Ross thought that was a little harsh, especially to those who had started early, because it seemed to be the adult thing to do. Additionally, this overlooked the influence of movies and television shows that portrayed smoking as a socially acceptable activity. For example, Roger Moore, *The Saint* in the 1960s television series, smoked. Ross once saw a smoking ad featuring actors from The Beverly Hillbillies and another made up from the cartoon characters of *The Flintstones*. Ross didn't know if either ad had ever made it to Australian television, but he strongly suspected they had played on American television; otherwise, they wouldn't have been made. He recalled the fictional Sergeant Fury from Marvel war comics with the cigar he permanently had lodged in his mouth.

When Ross asked Glenda about smoking, she told him she had tried it as a teenager but didn't like it, so she stopped doing it. Also, she thought it a grand waste of money.

Ross wasn't into heavy drug taking until he got both diabetes and cancer. The drugs he took were prescribed to him either by his local doctor or his cancer specialist. He was glad the government had subsidised them. Otherwise, he might not have been able to afford them. "All good," he told himself one day as he looked at all his pills. "They keep me alive, and nowadays, with my lady love, I have plenty to live for."

CHAPTER SEVENTEEN

Rain!

Ross Martin had never been a farmer, so he didn't have the appreciation some people had for what fell from the sky.

Australia had been drying up for millions of years. Whether white men with their industries had accelerated the process was something Ross didn't know. There would be a continuation of heavy rain, even flooding in the coastal areas at given times, but that's all. The large, permanent lake that early British-style explorers thought should be in the Centre didn't exist. The Aborigines were aware of this and had been so aware for a very long time. The system was against Ross having offspring; perhaps due to his continent's drying up. Why, then, is there a high rush to fill Australia with more and more migrants? It just didn't make sense. Maybe over time, people in high positions changed their minds? He supposed that was a possibility.

Most people live along the coast, and the weather can be unpredictable. By the time he reached voting age, Ross believed politicians couldn't read maps. There was talk of Australia becoming a large country in terms of population, despite its vast land area being mainly desert or semi-arid.

Ross could recall a sweltering summer in which he and his family, one day, were at Revesby Baths. A great crowd of people were there, and when it was time for the owner and his workers to close and send everyone away, the crowd, who were comfy in the water, refused to leave. They stayed, and the establishment did well in selling flavoured ice blocks. Overtime was paid to the workers, and the owner did all right, too. At midnight, when it rained, everyone in the various pools decided it was time to go.

Not all of Ross's childhood memories were bad. He had fond memories of those May trips up north on holiday. He remembered his father going to a house on the outskirts of Yamba, in northern New South Wales, to collect fresh honey from an old lady who kept bees in her backyard. It was a good, light, coastal-style honey, reflecting the kind of flowering plants found locally. These plants were hardy, able to stand up to the storms that came up and the days of tremendous sun in summer. The flowers tended to be minor, giving off a lovely perfume to attract the bees. The honey tasted best on fresh tank loaf bread with butter. It had been decades since Ross encountered that honey, but the taste remained.

Ross was aware of the decades-long droughts in New South Wales. One resulted in farmers joining the army as soldiers to aid the British in the Second Boer War (1899–1902). The money offered as pay was used to save the family farm.

In 1929, just as another drought had broken and there were good harvests in New South Wales, the Wall Street crash in the United States triggered the Great Depression, which affected Americans, the British, Australians, New Zealanders, the French, and the Germans. If not for the Great Depression, Hitler might never have gained power in Germany, and World War II might not have begun for the British and Australians in 1939.

In Ross's youth, there were stories of cats and dogs falling from the sky with the rain. He didn't believe that was at all possible. Tales of fish doing the same, he thought, might happen since he learned that water was drawn upward to once more fall, and fish live in water.

He recalled one trip up north with his parents and siblings during which it rained. They were in a cabin with a tin roof, and the rain coming down made a terrible racket. On that occasion, it was only for a day and a half, and it was sunny the rest of the time.

On another occasion, his dad had to pitch a tent in the rain. Ross and Ian did their best to help. The next day, it was sunny, which suited everyone.

Just before he met Glenda, he was told about the belief that water has memory. He not only found this hard to believe but was grateful it couldn't possibly be true. After all, the water he might be drinking out of a tap at home in Australia, or anywhere else for that matter, might have, centuries ago, passed through Napoleon's favorite horse, been drawn up into the sky numerous times and let down, been through the insides of countless people, to eventually end up in his drinking cup for him to consume. Ross concluded that it was better for water to have no memory.

He recalled a holiday where his dad could only get a week off work, so instead of heading north as usual, they went south to Sussex Inlet. There, it rained the entire week with a few hours, here and there, of calm but pending rain. During the calm, they would take a boat out to go fishing. Not much was caught. The only remarkable thing was when Kate, Ross's sister, landed a little green snake. She accidentally brought it into the boat, and it got off the hook and wriggled about. All on board feared being bitten by it, since no one knew if it was poisonous. Ross's dad used his boot and rod to corner and nudge it over the side. Everyone breathed a sigh of relief as they watched it swim toward the shore.

Could Sussex Inlet have been a great place to holiday if it hadn't rained so much? An uncle thought it was an excellent spot and had done well fishing there for bream and flathead. Of course, he had done so in better weather.

Ross recalled taking a train from Wellington in New South Wales to Sydney on a particularly steamy day close to Christmas. It was so hot that it affected the railroad tracks, forcing the train to go slowly. What further slowed the train was the decision of one young girl to give another young girl pierced ears as a present. It was done in the ladies' toilet, and something went wrong. An ambulance was called, and the train had to wait at the next station for the ambulance to arrive and take the girl away. *Why me?* Thought Ross at the time, hoping for rain that didn't come. He, of course, wasn't the only one inconvenienced or bothered by the weather or those silly girls.

One winter at college, he predicted snow but got sleet instead. One morning, he heard the crunch, crunch, crunch as he walked on the white covered grass.

While working for the railways, Ross got some good camera shots of lightning bolts coming down near a train station in the mid-west of New South Wales. The thunder that occurred moments later was terrific. The booming tingled the ears. However, there was no rain, although it came down the following day.

On another train trip, on a particularly muggy day in summer, he was grateful for a bit of rain to break up the heat. It came near the end of his shift, making sleeping that night much better.

Ross recalled the forest fires in New South Wales that devastated significant areas of natural growth and sent choking smoke south to districts not otherwise affected by the fires. The waterways began to dry up, and the smoke had made them more acidic. Fish floated to the surface dead. The only thing to do was pray for rain and be thankful when it came. There wasn't much that came that year, but there was enough, after weeks turned to months of drought, to aid firefighters in putting out the fires. Ross would never forget choking on the smoke as he lay in bed, wishing it would disappear. He was glad not to be in a position where he could easily have lost his unit. His place was a reasonable distance from large trees and bushland.

One year, it rained so heavily and for so long along the coast that it messed up communications on the internet, made the front and back lawns for weeks too wet to mow and ruined crops planted north of Sydney. Railway tracks were underwater, signal boxes were damaged, and roads were treacherous. Further north, close to the Queensland border and in Queensland itself, towns flooded out. Maclean, the most Scottish town in New South Wales, suffered water damage. This all came when COVID-19 was almost under control throughout New South Wales and other parts of Australia. Ross was in an excellent position to avoid having his home flooded, but he knew of people not far away doing it much more challenging than he was.

The rain continued into autumn. Autumn was always a time for coughs and colds anyway, and the cold and wet were bound to bring COVID-19 back with a vengeance. It did for a while, but the rain eased, and there was sunshine while going into a colder-than-usual winter. This mainly occurred on the east coast of New South Wales, with less rainfall inland.

CHAPTER EIGHTEEN

Poverty!

Australia isn't the worst country in the world for being poor. As Ross Martin discovered, you can always find someone worse off than you. There were times when he had only part-time work. The system crushed the unemployed and was not friendly to those with only part-time work.

Many years later, after beating the system, he could look back on those years and find them helpful. They made him stronger in ways he would appreciate when his life finally came together, as he had often dreamed it would. He admitted he now ate better than at other times when he didn't have much money. Glenda saw to that, and he ensured she ate well, too. The retirement years were then the best, but some moments made them even better.

Full-time employment, lasting for a decade, should have been a bonus in making the system work for him for a change. The fact that it couldn't do so meant something. How influential was this system, and why was it so against him? He understood that it was tied to modern living and required a person to have courage at the right time. It had to do with religion of one kind or another messing about with one's head.

Ross hadn't always had the luxury of a job that suited him. When that job came along, he held onto it with both hands and could not see himself jeopardising it over what he thought would be the slim possibility of dating an office woman. Why ask a woman out when, according to the office heads, he had no right to do so, and if it ever got out that he had done so, he'd be finished? Putting his fate into the hands of a person he hardly knew, for the sake of maybe getting to know her better, did not make any sense.

Near the end of his time as an office worker, Ross bought his unit. His sister, Kate, had talked him into it, and it was a good decision. Instead of renting forever, he had a place to pay off and live in. It took him twenty years to do so because of unsteady work, but it belonged to him once that was done. The only snag was the corporate body and its demands for more money. It was a two-bedroom dwelling, and he used the second bedroom to store all the stuff he had collected over the years.

Was a structure created in the mid-1970s ancient? Ross didn't think so, but some disagreed with that view. It was a ground-floor dwelling with a tiny hot water system for showers and baths. The nearest beach was half a mile away, and the closest train station was just three hundred yards away. It suited him quite well until he met the love of his life and came to live with her closer to a beach.

With the cost of fuel and maintenance rising and him without a steady job, he could no longer afford the upkeep of his automobile. Thus, it was a sad day when he had to sell the last car he would ever own.

Ross enjoyed working for the railway. It didn't pay much, and the work wasn't consistent, but he liked the people he was with. He was employed at various times to do all sorts of things on the trains and stations. He travelled as far north as Newcastle and as far south as Nowra. He inspected trains and train stations to ensure they were in good condition and counted the number of passengers. Sometimes, in winter, he froze at some of the stations he was at. One was tough in winter because of the cool breeze from the ocean and the chilly air from the nearby cemetery. No matter how well he rugged up, he froze. He was glad to be young enough not to care.

Sometimes, he worked at night on the trams and the trains. At Central in winter, he noticed the tents on the green near the railway station. The occupants were the homeless who had nowhere else to sleep. There were also roaming rats that came out after dark. He promised himself he would never find himself in that situation where he had to hope a rat didn't decide to invade his makeshift home. He also saw the occasional rat on the train lines of Town Hall and other underground stations. *People shouldn't throw their garbage onto the tracks*, he thought one night while waiting for a train home. He was watching a rat inspecting an empty packet of crisps for sustenance.

It was sad, but some people slept as best they could on the trains and washed up in the toilets at various stations. Some shop owners gave them food. Usually, they would otherwise throw out the leftovers. Some lacked intelligence, while one old woman Ross met was a university professor who had dropped out of society and enjoyed the freedom of the vagabond life. Her domain was the wild places, and she could always get a meal somewhere. It wasn't the kind of existence that would ever be a lure for Ross, but that was okay. He had his books, DVDS, and his unit. He wasn't prepared to give them up, though others might choose to do so. Even so, he had to admire the spirit of someone who gave up everything for what she told him was a better life.

This old woman had a different attitude toward Muslims. She once told him their take on the family was better than that of Christians. He couldn't see that himself and wondered how she could arrive at that conclusion. She also thought Agatha Christie was a terrible writer. Ross agreed that *Murder on the Orient Express* was a cheat because virtually everyone on the train was involved in the crime. The joy of a 'who-done-it' for most readers was working out from clues who the killer happened to be. Many years later, Agatha Christie's stage play *Mouse Trap* came to Sydney, and he found it enjoyable.

Ross remembered being allowed in the train driver's compartment once and seeing the trip through the underground tunnels on the Sydney Circle from the train driver's point of view. There were coloured lights that meant nothing to Ross, but he knew from the driver that those lights provided lots of information.

There were rare occasions when a train broke down in one of the tunnels of the Sydney City Circle, and it took a couple of hours to not only get it functioning again and out of the tunnel but to resume regular traffic flow. He knew it made for a long day for railway personnel. One afternoon, he was stuck in Sydney for a couple of hours.

It was train travel that got him back to photography. When working at a train station to do counts, he got there before he had to start, and he sometimes had as much as an hour to kill after his shift. What was he to do with that time? Finding something to eat didn't take much time since pie shops and hamburger joints tended to be close to train stations. What was there to do then when he wasn't working or eating? The mobile phone he had on him was the answer. He could take photos with it and discovered that all the stations he visited had something unique about them worth photographing. Eventually, he acquired a new digital camera, allowing him to take better pictures.

After his part-time job with the railway petered out, he continued taking photos. By then, he had turned to wildlife photography and joined a birders club. He was to continue with wildlife photography for the rest of his life.

In his old age, he recalled friendships with railway workers that had lasted for decades. He didn't get along with all station managers, but he did get along with most of them, plus his fellow workers, guards, and train drivers.

Ross worked in a library for a time. It was pleasant. He liked the smell of books, and when he was on duty cataloguing old photographs, he enjoyed that too. He also learned what people were interested in reading and why. Westerns were popular in that library.

When Ross worked for a food producer, it was all about getting everything done efficiently and being able to buy food at a low cost as a bonus. A doctor was on the site, and Ross had to have a medical check every time he got a few weeks of work. There came a day when the doctor made him a cup of coffee, asked if he had felt ill since the previous week when he had been examined and then let him trot off to the factory floor. He had to admit she had a delightful sense of the absurd.

Ross recalled a story he was told about a man who had a lawn mowing concern way back in the 1980s. He and his crew mowed the lawns of government greens as well as the grass of homeowners. When Work for the Dole came about, it was decided that government greens could now be mowed at a cheaper cost by those on the dole. And so, the man with his lawn mowing concern found he couldn't get enough business just mowing the grass of householders. He and his crew went out of business and onto the dole. What did he have to do for the dole, you ask? He and his crew had to mow government lawns for less than the minimum wage.

In Exile!

Before meeting Glenda, his lovely lady, Ross Martin had moments in his unit where he would touch his hand with his other hand and imagine what it would be like if the other hand belonged to someone else. A pretty someone at that. He also imagined what it would be like to have plenty of money and be known as a fine fellow. The system was designed to keep him lonely and unimportant. Sure, he had family, but they had their own lives, and he didn't want to bother them too much.

He read somewhere that you could make a fist and, in moving your mouth over it, get some idea of what kissing a woman on the lips would be like. It seemed silly, but he tried it and found it unsatisfactory. Sometimes, he was close enough to Penelope to smell strawberries on her lips, and he found this more to his liking.

Ross spent much of his childhood either buried in books or watching television. He had isolated himself, and the system was delighted to use this against him in the coming years.

Then Muslims came to Australia in vast numbers. He had enough trouble with Christianity. He thought Islam was better for men but not suitable for his sister and his other female acquaintances. If it was no good for them, it ultimately was not good for humanity. And if it was no good for humanity, then it was no good for civilisation. He understood that Muslim countries that were not oil-rich were impoverished.

At college, he studied in his room and the library. He discovered that famous 19th-century British and American writers often did not start as geniuses in the art of literature. There was a writing curve to greatness, which he found inspirational. He didn't have to be great to start. He just had to keep improving as he continued to write.

Charles Dickens' earlier novels had a touch too much of the soap to them. *A Christmas Carol* and other short Christmas stories by Dickens, except *The Battle of Life*, Ross thought of as brilliant. *Oliver Twist* told Ross he wasn't so bad off living in 20th-century Australia. Dickens was a reformer and wanted children from deplorable backgrounds in England to have a better start in life. Dickens had a rough childhood, so he knew firsthand what he was writing about.

Before coming to college, Ross had read *1984* by George Orwell, which challenged the very nature of the society in which he lived. Were wars inevitable because they could keep politicians in power? Can history be altered to satisfy the government of the day? Where was the truth then about whether such things could happen? This question became more profound in the 1990s with the rise of political correctness and in the early 21st Century with the emergence of Black Lives Matter and the concept of "woke." It seemed to Ross that Woke was all about praising minorities and a kick in the bum to anyone who didn't belong to a minority. Still, in the early 21st Century, Ross was a minority of one, which didn't get him anywhere. Of course, his minority was never likely to be recognised by the Woke folk.

Among the plays that were on the shelves of the college library, there was one that caught his attention. It was translated from Russian and dates back to the 1920s. The cover was unimpressive, but that didn't matter. Lots of plays had lousy covers. It was a fantasy set in medieval times where a red dragon terrorised a town. The townsfolk hire a knight in white armour to slay the dragon. The knight heads off to do so, but along the way, comes up with a bright idea. The townsfolk could pay him for one dead dragon or keep paying him to chase off the dragon. So, he made a deal with the dragon, and the dragon and the knight profited from the arrangement.

Ross figured the red dragon represented the Red Army, the communists, and the white knight, the White Army, the Democrats. The playwright shows both as bad as each other. Of course, the Red Army eventually won the Civil War in the 1920s, but feeding an army, regardless of which one, took a heavy toll on Russian farmers of the time. He could imagine a Russian village first plundered by the Red Army and then by the Whites.

Throughout history, the Russians had done it much more challenging than Ross's people. Communism as an ideal was OK, but it could not put food on the table like capitalism could. Was capitalism perfect? No. But it was more flexible than Russian-style communism, and therein lay its strength. Also, many people need to believe in a god, a goddess or a collection of deities, and communism was opposed to any such worship. Hence, even at communism's height in Russia, underground Christian groups were meeting in secret, only revealing themselves when strictures on religion had eased.

Ross, in his old age, remembered the arms race of the 1960s and 1970s. It was possible back then to have an all-out war with Russia and possibly Red China and lose everything. Great mushroom clouds everywhere. Everything is blown up or torn down—melting steel and glass. Civilisation gone. Someone howling in the wind for food. Cans contaminated. Water radioactive. The soil is useless. Maybe New Zealand would be spared, and possibly parts of Norway. Not so Australia, due to its ties to the USA. The UK is a wasteland.

Ross read that there were some Americans, in the 1950s going into the 1960s, who had bomb shelters built to protect themselves and their families from first atomic and then nuclear devastation. He didn't think these shelters would do much good since, sooner or later, those in them would have to leave and take their chances anyway. He couldn't imagine the ones he had seen holding more than a couple of months' worth of food and water for a family. He thought contamination from radiation over the land would likely last much longer than a few months.

Comics produced in the USA, such as Slow Death, made all this apparent. Ross kept one of them. The writers and artists proclaimed that the arms race could only end in disaster. Also, its expense was crippling parts of the USA and Russia. People were going without what they needed for weapons that must never be used.

Perhaps, because the Russians were communist and, therefore, presumably not religious, the final battle with the USA and other Western powers was never going to happen. None wanted a complete wipeout. To threaten was one thing, but to deliver, knowing the enemy would swiftly retaliate, was another. Religion would have made the difference, or so Ross thought, reflecting on Muslims strapping bombs to themselves to blow up the people they saw as the enemy. There had to be paradise awaiting you, at least in your thought processes, to thus end your life and that of others.

The James Bond movies continued past 1989 but were never as humorous or action-packed, with the world's fate in balance, as they had been earlier. By the 21st century, they were limping and had little to say about current world conditions since they could not be mentioned without the movies being closed. Ross thought of the books, still coming out past Ian Fleming's lifetime, as better put together and retained a sense of Bond being able to save at least a small portion of his world.

By the time Ross entered college and found that Russian play from the 1920s, no one believed anymore that the conflict between Russia and the USA would ever heat up to the point of destruction of everything. The Cold War between the USA and Russia had been too cold for too long for that to occur. No one on either side would start something that had to end in utter destruction.

By the 1980s, the fictional British agent James Bond was no longer needed to stop the USA and Russia from blowing everything up. In 1989, peace was achieved between the USA and Russia. There would be fewer nuclear missiles in the world, and countries such as Poland would not need to remain communist.

In terms of *1984* and that Russian play, Ross, in college, wondered just how well he fitted into the dynamics of the society he was living in. It was capitalist and democratic with a touch of socialism. He concluded that, despite his best efforts, he didn't do well at all. He was already a loner with few friends, and that would be his continuing fate for quite some time.

After college, Ross met up with some artists and, to save money, shared a house with them. This worked out fine for a while. They shared their interest in music with him, but film and photography were always his bag. Even so, he got the impression from them that music had developed over the years and was still developing.

He discovered from them that Punk became popular in the UK when there was high unemployment among young people. He also learned that some Punk bands eventually turned to New Wave. Punk, Ross understood he could only appreciate from a historical perspective as protest music. New Wave was more to his liking.

Later, Ross shared a house with a woman around his age and her son. This was a huge mistake! His music friends warned him against doing so, but unfortunately, the warnings didn't take effect. He wasn't suited to having a scatterbrained teen in his life who curtailed the freedom of home he so cherished.

During the working week, he had an hour's train ride in the morning and again in the afternoon. There, on the train, he could read and write. When he returned to his digs, he wanted a hot shower, a go on his computer, some television, and to read for a while before going to sleep. These things had been denied to him. The computer made a noise, inevitably leading to a knock on the door to his bedroom and a long conversation he didn't want to have while trying to relax. There was a way of turning hot water into cold water by simply turning on other taps in the house. This was how he was deprived of a decent shower. *Even prisoners in jail are entitled to a hot shower*, he thought to himself glumly when this happened to him.

He went to a local pub to drink beer and read one afternoon. It was better than going straight back to his digs, or so he thought. He did this a couple more times. Then, a local journalist warned him at the bar that the alcoholics were not too happy with him reading in their pub. That night, he was mugged of sixty dollars on his walk back to his residence. He reported it to the police, but nothing came of it. He never returned to that pub, and he would not have been sorry if someone had blown it up with those barflies still inside.

He had to get out, and after he did so, he would not share dwellings with anyone permanently for decades. First, he rented independently; then, he bought a unit by himself. For over a year, it was glorious being by himself.

When Ross was out of full-time work and living in his unit, he was neither willing nor wealthy enough to spend much money on going out. He had been poorly stung by living with that terrible woman and her son. For years afterwards, he basked in being alone.

Being alone, he could do whatever he pleased in his own space. He felt hard done by that he hadn't had this space all to himself earlier with money in his pocket, but at least he had it now. He told himself some life lessons are brutal, reflecting on that woman and her son. It would be decades before he would again share a place with anyone, but when he did, Glenda, his loving woman, helped turn it into a home.

CHAPTER TWENTY

What are His Rights?

For two years of his life, thanks to Glenda Evens, Ross Martin didn't have to wonder about his rights as a human being. Glenda had aided him in defeating the system, and as far as he was concerned, all was as close to being right with the world as the world could be. Until then, he questioned why others seemed to have more rights than he possessed. Good looks and money, he understood, came into it, but he also realised there was more than that going on. There was the bad boy versus the good guy business.

Ross had to admit he would always be the good guy, whatever that might mean to others. He couldn't help himself. Maybe it had something to do with the American comic books he had read as a boy. He liked to feel heroic, but, at the same time, realised the bad guys in movies tended to do all right up until the end when the hero wins. Could that be how life works? Maybe he was only expected to win in the end.

"Next lifetime, I will be the villain," Ross said to himself one day in the mirror. Then I have all those years of excellent bastardry before getting caught and answering for my numerous sins."

He didn't think life operated like a B-grade film, but he was tickled by the notion that it just might do so and that he was foolish not to put on the black hat for a while and have fun.

The USA and the United Nations had it that we are all entitled to life, liberty, and the pursuit of happiness. There is no guarantee that you will achieve happiness; however, you will be entitled to pursue it. For Ross Martin, the system was against such actions unless you could act without getting caught. If not, you were forbidden, and you could be punished for even thinking of putting your skates on and running after your desires. By pursuing, you could be stepping on someone else's happiness, which would never do. The more he thought about it, the more complicated the whole damn thing became. He understood that some women took a fellow wanting to go beyond friendship as a betrayal. He found this hard to understand, as all she had to do was say 'no, thank you' and return to being his friend.

Ross found what happiness he could in objects, such as books and DVDs, rather than people, because humans were just too complicated. He didn't like trying to date because of the possible melodrama. He gathered that if he had had the right friends when he was younger, perhaps something could have been sorted out, but by the time he went to college, his lack of knowledge made him uncomfortable, and he stumbled about.

He wanted to know what was right and wrong in the mating game. At age thirty, he was expected to know more than he could. Pretending that he did have broader knowledge was disastrous. When he was in college, he wanted to tell his fellow college students how he had lost a decade by looking too young, but he felt that sounded weak, even if it was true.

Ross's brother, Ian, dared to pursue happiness in his late teens and won. In quick time, a girlfriend became a mother and then a wife. It wasn't all easygoing for Ian, as Ross initially thought. There were money concerns. Ross's dad had to help. Even so, Ian had got the jump on his older brother, and that was that.

Ross could have been kinder to his brother about this sudden marriage, but all he could feel was the loss of being unable to marry first and the realisation that marriage might never happen for him. The system had chosen Ian over Ross, which had been the case for a long time.

When in college, Penelope entered Ross's life and things, women-wise, weren't so bad. He hoped to make it with her. This didn't happen, but at least he had her as a friend. He was surprised at how long their friendship would last. In some ways, she was the wild child he could never be. She was an Aquarius, and he was a Capricorn. Maybe if they had mated, their friendship wouldn't have lasted. Perhaps she was afraid that after sex, he'd cling to her, and she didn't want anyone doing that. Would he have done so? He didn't think so, but he honestly didn't know.

In Australia in the 1970s, there was considerable discussion about women's rights in society. It seemed fair enough to Ross that if a woman does the same work as a man, she should get the same pay rate. This wasn't always so in the past, but became more so at that juncture. What did this personally have to do with Ross Martin? Very little at first until his mother had to take a part-time job to make ends meet. Ross and his siblings were called upon to help more around the house. This took more convincing than it should have because Ross thought of going to school as his job and housework as his mother's duties.

Ross's sister, Kate, supported women's liberation even though neither she nor Ross initially understood it. It seemed like a good idea to her and a questionable one to him. Why couldn't life continue the way it always had?

The answer was in Ross's grandfather on his father's side, who had a stroke in his efforts to hold down two jobs. He had done this to prevent his wife and children from starving. He had battled to keep his family financially solvent during the difficult years of the Great Depression, when jobs were scarce and didn't always pay well enough. As Ross's father took on the role of husband and provider, he believed the wife looked after the home and the children, and the husband went out to work. He felt defeated when his job wasn't enough, and his wife had to contribute financially to keep his home and family together. Like many other husbands, he got over it because he had to do so.

It was strange, but inflation climbed when Australia went from pounds, shillings and pence to dollars and cents. As a child, Ross was aware that you could get more lollies with a shilling than with a ten-cent piece. Also, the price of American comic books rose from twelve cents to fifteen and then to twenty. The Australian pound used to do well against the American dollar. Then, after the conversion, the Australian dollar performed poorly. Around this time, tariffs were eliminated, which meant the end of several industries since labour and materials were cheaper elsewhere. What this meant to most households was the need for a second income and workers to hold onto their factory work for as long as possible.

Later, Kate told Ross how much their mother enjoyed working as a seamstress again. She did it before her marriage and had fond memories of welcoming the soldiers home from the 2nd World War with cuttings tossed out of the top window in Sydney, where she was employed, down to them like coloured streamers. She liked getting out of the house and having some other purpose than looking after kids and the home. It was an adjustment the whole family made in the 1970s, and there was no going back to the previous way of life.

In the ensuing years, there was a lot of talk about women's rights. Ross couldn't always see where they were hard done by. In the office where he worked, the glass ceiling people continually talked about on television didn't exist, and it was not there in the library or on the railway. *It must be somewhere*, he thought. *I don't know where!* Then he met up with a cousin who told him she had missed a promotion at a bank because she was a woman. *There!* He thought. *Now, I finally know where this glass ceiling can be found.*

Going to discos, he wondered what his rights were and whether they existed. His sister, Kate, didn't think they were necessary since he was a man. There seemed to be the belief that he had it all, being a male, but what did he have?

In the program set in America, *Mad Men*, Ross understood the 20th-century nature of advertising on television and elsewhere. It had been discovered that women did most of the shopping, and therefore, they were the primary target when new products came onto the market. Why cater exclusively for men when women were doing the purchasing? Even items used mainly by men were chiefly bought by women. Empowering women, then, was one answer the advertisers came up with. What's more, what was good in the USA and the UK was also good for Australia.

Ross remembered board game ads on television around Christmas time. If it were just a husband and wife playing, the wife would win. If a husband, wife, son, and daughter were playing, the daughter would win.

He recalled safety ads in which the boy is naughty, but the girl does the right thing. It reminded him of what, in a nursery rhyme, girls were supposed to be made of: sugar, spice, and all that's nice. Meanwhile, boys were said to be fashioned out of snips and snails and puppy-dog tails. This singing endorsement for girls originated from an earlier century, alongside a less-than-complimentary view of boys. Even so, it stuck and was still being touted in the 1960s and 1970s. Since Ross was once a boy, was there a snail in his DNA? He didn't believe this to be the case since, in his youth, he could be fast on his feet.

In primary school, playground bullies couldn't touch him when he put on the speed. He suspected that someone chased him to see him run. In high school, he thought he might be okay at track, but others were better than he was at running, and he never received proper training to improve.

One of Ross's nephews had the good looks of his father but also his dad's talent for getting mixed up with attractive but loopy women. It was as if he were born with this golden ticket but had no idea how to use it. Ross didn't know whether to envy him or feel sorry for him. Between disasters, this fellow no doubt had a good time.

There was a young woman with whom this nephew bought a house, and then something happened between them, and she was gone. This meant he had a mortgage he couldn't handle on his own, and his parents had to rescue him. On another occasion, a young Muslim woman wanted to marry him to get away from her parents. That quickly fell through, and he was undoubtedly lucky that it did, since he was headed for a culture clash. After a while, Ross lost track of him and his adventures, and maybe that was for the best.

This fellow's father had married a woman with some weird ideas about Ross, which he found upsetting. By age 21, he didn't want to spend time alone with her. He took her to be one of the beautiful people with absolutely no fundamental understanding of how others, such as himself, lived, nor was she indeed capable of such an understanding. She thought she knew him, but she was wrong.

Back when he was ten, she was pretty. By the time he was 21, she was still striking, with a good figure, but by then, he and Ross's father found her sanity questionable. She had a lot of sympathy for Ross, whom he found poisonous. It all began with a pair of winter pyjamas given to him by her one Christmas. It was a crazy gift for a ten-year-old, especially during an Australian summer. Even so, his mother urged Ross to be grateful for it, and he did his best. Maybe he was too appreciative, which gave this silly creature the idea that he bizarrely was into clothes. His sister, Kate, was also given strange presents by her, but she was not asked to make anything out of them, so that she may have been protected in that way. He forgot what that woman gave his brother, Ian, that Christmas. What he did know was that Ian, possibly because of his stockiness, was not to be in for any demoralising sympathy from their nutty aunt.

Ross's uncle had a sports car and a lovely home. His bizarre wife thought she was an artist, so she had her paintings on the walls. It took little time for Ross to forget what the paintings were about, so he realised, in hindsight, they mustn't have been excellent. Either that or he wasn't a great judge of abstract art.

Ross's 21st was a disaster as parties go, with the keg of beer supplied for the occasion flat and undrinkable. The fact that this woman was there, dripping with her nutty sympathy, worsened matters. Years later, when she had grown large in places and was no longer considered pretty, he began to feel sorry for her and the man she had married. Both could have been catwalk models with that sports car when he was ten, giving them a James Bond appeal. His uncle would have been lucky if she had been more sensible.

Ross was once shown a photo of how his uncle looked when he was ten. He compared it with a picture of himself at ten, and there were similarities. Unfortunately, Ross didn't turn out stately and tall like his uncle, but short and weedy like his father.

Why couldn't I have been blessed like my uncle? Ross thought on one occasion. *But with a keener understanding of women? Maybe the sharper understanding my dad once had would be enough if only I had that.*

Ross knew he was better off than people living in some other countries. In the 1990s, he learned that Australia's minimum wage was higher than America's, allowing one to live on it. He also knew that waiters in Australia didn't have to rely on tips to make a living. Meanwhile, Ethiopia experienced severe droughts, and starvation was a constant threat. Indeed, in the 1970s, Aboriginal Australians were doing it tough. Government funds were allocated to address that problem, but they didn't always reach the people who needed help. In the early 21st Century, more money was supposed to go to helping out Aborigines, but no one except those in the know could say where this money went. Some Aboriginal communities were doing reasonably well.

In the 1990s, a writer friend of Ross's decided to enter an arranged marriage. He went to the Philippines, found the woman he wanted, and took her back to Australia to marry him. Soon after this occurred, Ross lost contact with him, so he had no idea how it worked out. He did, however, tell Penelope about it one day over lunch at a restaurant.

"You're not thinking of doing that, are you?" she asked Ross.

"I couldn't afford to do it even if I wanted to," he told her.

"Would you if you could?" she asked.

"I don't know," said Ross.

"It's like buying someone," she told him, frowning. "Nothing good can come of it."

"I suppose you are right," he answered, then wondered if that was correct. There was the possibility of a grand and continuing sex life if only he had the money and the will to get it started. Was it too daring for him? He thought it might be.

Ross imagined going to the Philippines, bedding a young woman, taking her back to Australia, marrying her there, and her becoming an Australian citizen. What might then follow? Divorce, and half of whatever he has is going to her. It could happen.

He knew he didn't know the culture in the Philippines at all, and taking advantage of someone might quickly go wrong, and he would be out of pocket and with nothing much to show for it. Even if she was a decent person, a relationship built on his lust and desire to be alone no longer stood much of a chance of working out long-term. Making someone a slave, even for a short while, was not something he ever wanted to do. Whether others liked it or not, he had a right to be alone and to contemplate a better ending to his loneliness than that.

At the same time, women in Russia were seeking men in the USA, Australia, and Canada to marry. Still, Ross was not interested, especially after his talk with Penelope. From Russia with love, he thought of as too distant a possibility. He wasn't James Bond. Marriage to someone he didn't know, wherever they came from, was too risky, even if the money was there to take his chances with her.

A decade later, he came across an Australian movie comedy in which a naïve Australian fellow marries a Russian woman who turns out to be a Russian prostitute on the run from a Russian gang and finds refuge with him in Sydney. The Russian gang ends up in Sydney, and, between gunshots, the naïve Australian fellow must decide if he loves her or not, and she has to discover if she can love him.

He also watched an episode of *A Country Practice* in which an Indonesian woman is brought to Australia and then mistreated by the Australian brute she has married. Did such things go on? He imagined they might. He had no desire to bring anyone to his country just so he could mistreat them, and he did not want to be mistreated.

In old age, Ross had found someone who could be both a friend and a lover, without the baggage attached. Whatever baggage he had accumulated over time, he could also throw away. He was no longer a victim of the system and had no need or desire to victimise someone else. It was such a strange business being on such good terms with someone. He was rich in ways he had never been before.

CHAPTER TWENTY-ONE

You Must be Politically Correct!

Ross Martin understood that in the 1990s, a communist spirit was abroad. It tapped into the system. It was promoted by the great universities in England and the USA by well-meaning, though rather stupid, academics. It was called political correctness, and the general idea, in the beginning, was to change how people think by changing their words. If they had only read *1984* by George Orwell, they might have thought twice about that venture. Around this same time, some turned Big Brother into a so-called reality show, thus blunting the teeth of *1984*.

As Ross understood from his college studies, the universities of England had a long history of communist activity dating back to the 1930s. Such activities were tolerated in the 1940s because the Soviet Union was a crucial ally in the war against Germany. In the 1950s, there was a crackdown against it in the UK, the USA and Australia. Anyone who appeared to be Red was blacklisted in the USA from television and the movies. Something similar happened in Britain and Australia, but as far as Ross understood, not as much fuss was made about doing so.

Ross learned at college that John Wayne was very anti-communist in the 1950s and in favor of having writers and actors with communist backgrounds blacklisted. His support of the Vietnam War was not appreciated by college kids facing the draft. What came to light was that Wayne had made numerous war movies but had never served in the US military. In other words, he had been urging others to risk their lives for their country but had never done so himself.

Communism went underground during the Cold War era but resurfaced, first as political correctness, then in the early 21st Century as Black Lives Matter, and finally, as Woke. In all its incarnations, it promised everything to its followers and delivered very little to anyone in return. It could never get past the need for people to sell and buy goods. It could not wholly undermine patriotism or prevent the truth about the past from being revealed.

In the office of the 1990s, complimenting co-workers of the opposite sex could be dangerous. This had everything to do with political correctness. Ross recalled a current affairs program in which, to fill up airtime, an interviewer went into a typical office and urged the people there to flirt with one another. Some of the women did so, but none of the men. They all knew better. Whatever they might say, no matter how weak and seemingly inoffensive, would later come back to bite them and there, on television, would be proof of their misdeed, whatever it might be. There is a lot of shaking of heads by the men and sympathetic looks given to them by the women. The interviewer seemed oblivious to what was going on around her.

If a man at an office in the 1990s dared compliment a woman on her haircut or anything else, he was, from a politically correct standpoint, asking for trouble. It was called objectivizing. Women could do it, but not most men.

Ross grew up on non-politically correct shows such as *Benny Hill, Paul Hogan, Love Thy Neighbour, D Generation, Fast Forward,* and *Kingswood*

Country. In the 21ˢᵗ Century, such programs would be considered too offensive to be shown on television, but they would end up as clips on YouTube for him to enjoy.

Then there was *Monty Python's Flying Circus*, an English show where anything and everything could happen, from silly walks to Vikings singing about spam. Nudity and general naughtiness were also part of the show.

The political correctness monster was already making inroads into television when the company that made Love Thy Neighbour in England set a few episodes in Australia. No doubt, the writers were given a list of things they couldn't make fun of, which resulted in the show lacking teeth and, thus, having no reason to exist.

Ross grew up with the British Carry-On films, regarding them as fun and not to be taken too seriously. They often appeared on Australian television during school holidays. The women and men in these movies seemed as naïve as Ross frequently felt himself to be. His favourites were *Carry-On Cleo* and *Carry-On Screaming.* Cleo was a send-up of Roman, Egyptian, and British history. Screaming was a tongue-in-cheek salute to Hammer horror. Were they sexist? Ross didn't think so. Were they rude? Yes.

Some of the young women at college hated the Carry-On films. He gathered they didn't like the suggestiveness of some of the lines of dialogue in them.

Ross recalled that the last of the Carry-ons was unwatchable because the laughs were no longer there. The innuendos were no longer naughty. What they were, he didn't understand, nor did he like. It was as if the knack of making them and doing it right, or at any rate to his satisfaction, had somehow been lost.

In the 1970s, there was a martial arts craze headed by Bruce Lee. There were dozens of action-packed movies. *Enter the Dragon* (1973) was one of the best. With them, Ross recalled a comedy about a less-than-brilliant martial artist in which this fellow says in a poster caption: "I am a sex object. When I ask for sex, the women object." He never did get to see the movie, but those lines stuck in his head. Just who is a sex object anyway? All creatures that are sexual rather than asexual happen to be attractive to someone. Men are attracted to women, and women are attracted to men, and there are other attractions.

In Wales, early in the 21st Century, a disgruntled diner reported an eatery on the internet for supporting blackface. On one of its walls, the eatery had an old photo of coal miners with soot on their clothing and faces from working in a coal mine. The owner was undoubtedly proud of his family members who had mined for coal. Ross picked this story up on YouTube.

One program Ross knew about that would have ticked off the Woke crowd into a rage if aired in the 21st Century was *The Black and White Minstrel Show.* Made in the UK with black face, white gloves, dance and song from the USA's deep south, it could not be argued that it was just some variety form of entertainment. Back in the 1960s, Ross found it boring. The fact that it had lasted on the air a long time meant someone liked it.

Ross noted that there weren't many shows on television in the 1960s and 1970s that dealt with Australian Aboriginal issues other than the news and sport. One was Skippy, and the other was The Magic Boomerang. A Country Practice came later in the 1980s. For Black Lives Matter and then Woke, Aboriginal rights were fertile ground. There had been Aboriginal deaths in custody in the 1990s that had, understandably, led to outrage in some Australian communities.

In September of 2001, the USA mainland was attacked by Muslim terrorists. Ross recalled seeing the Twin Towers in New York demolished on television. The next day, going to work via train, he noticed American visitors in tears being comforted by Australians who were just as shocked by what had happened in New York and Washington. *Are they insane?* Ross thought about the terrorists as he got off the train. *They won't get what they want, whatever the hell that is!*

Years later, there was an attempt by American Muslims to build a Muslim youth and prayer centre where the Twin Towers in New York had stood. Protests from everywhere, including Ross on the internet, put a stop to that! He and many others thought it was disrespectful. But the very audacity of such a plan meant there would be continuing hatred for Muslims in the USA and elsewhere, despite the innocence of most Muslims over what Americans now call 9/11.

Some wars came out of 9/11, not only involving Americans but also the British and the Australians as well.

Ross was renting in Cronulla in 2002, at the time of the Bali Bombings. He didn't know any of the surfers who had gone to Bali, in Indonesia, for a holiday, only to get murdered by fanatical Muslims out to teach both the West and Balinese Hindus a lesson in bloodshed and violence. Like many people living in the area, he was shocked that this could happen for no good reason. There was a Balinese shop owner in Cronulla who pleaded with the locals not to hate her. She was in tears and was comforted by them. She and the locals had lost people, so there was shared sympathy. Other townships in Australia had also lost young people, but Ross only knew about the ones in Cronulla, even though he understood the loss had been more widespread.

A short while later, one of the bombers was arrested, and he was there, in a jail cell, smiling at the camera as if he had done something he had every right to be proud of. The jailer was also smiling, which irked Ross. Why was he behaving this way? Was the jailor on the side of his prisoner? This didn't seem right. What did a bunch of kids in their late teens, off on a surfing holiday in Bali, ever do to deserve to be blown up?

Nothing, as far as Ross was concerned. To this day, there is a memorial near the sea at Cronulla in memory of the young women whose lives had been cut short by Indonesian terrorists.

In 2005, there was the Cronulla riot. Ross understood that there had been, for years, tensions between local surfers and Muslim youth who rode the rails from Bankstown to Cronulla. Because of this, a Greek Australian artist friend felt unwelcome in that town. Generally, this had nothing to do with anyone who wasn't a local surfer or a Muslim youth. If it had stayed that way, tensions might have eased, even disappeared over time, and everything would have been fine. Unfortunately, this did not happen.

Ross found out later that the police were made helpless to act earlier because of political correctness. They could not be seen to be racist, even acting in support of order against what was evident to the locals as being a Muslim youth form of racism.

As hostile feelings continued to rise, young women were hassled on the beaches by, no doubt, self-righteous Muslims for wearing bikinis. Then, a lifesaver, after saving a Muslim woman from drowning, was punched by a Muslim youth for touching her.

It was hoped that a peaceful protest would return stability to Cronulla if only the public knew what was happening, but that was not the case. The anger boiled over into attacks on both the innocent and the guilty. A Sikh couple, who had visited the beaches for over a decade, harming none, were driven away, mistaken for Muslims, despite being dressed like Sikhs.

Ross was there and had to agree that the Muslim youth present was only getting what they deserved, but at the cost of everyone else's sanity. They were the actual racists but were later labelled as the victims instead by television. A documentary was released that irked Ross by doing so. It thus took him a while to realise that not all Muslims living in Australia are bad and that some of them, if not most of them, are decent, friendly folk. The terrorist attack in 2013 in the USA at the Boston Marathon did not help, nor did the Lindt Café siege in Sydney in 2014 or the Manchester Arena bombing in the UK in 2017.

In the end, Ross had to remind himself that Christians could also be fanatically evil, though he didn't know of any that had tried to blow himself and others up in the name of their religion. He was familiar, however, with the Crusades and how nut jobs joined the Knights Templar to obtain salvation with the sword. Also, there was how Christian belief, with its no sex before marriage, had clashed mightily in his life with the hippy notion of making love, not war, resulting in no woman for him, no wife and no offspring.

The message given by the Woke people in the early 21st Century, after much hand wringing, seemed to be, to Ross, a case of if you are brown, stick around, but if you are white, get out of sight. Was this racist? No, because according to the Woke experts, only white men could be that way inclined. No one else could be racist.

Ross recalled a woman, way back in the 1990s, on an American program, saying that white women with racist husbands go along with their husbands and are not themselves racist. Ross thought this was the greatest copout and later realised how it could be spun for political and Woke reasons.

He looked up the term "woke" in the 2020 Oxford Dictionary and was informed that it meant being alert to societal injustice, especially racism. It also noted that being woke was pretentious about how much you care about a social issue. The last bit he could easily confirm.

If you can't find a social issue, make one up, Ross thought while wincing at an episode of *Star Trek Discovery*. Spock could no longer be the logical half-man and half-Vulcan of earlier *Star Trek*. That had to be given over to someone else, less white.

Ross followed the adventures of Spock from *Star Trek*, the original series, onward. He had two hundred original novels and was looking forward to the television series *Star Trek: Discovery*. Then, when he saw how the writers on that show had peeled away Spock's logic and intelligence in the name of diversity, he had to shake his head and stop watching. The show was just too Woke for him to stomach.

From his history studies, he knew that during the Elizabethan age in England, upper-class sophisticates would add powder containing arsenic and other poisons to their faces to achieve the whitest complexion possible. It also gave them a buzz. By the early 21st Century, however, in the name of Woke solidarity, college and university students wanted to be as dark as possible to escape the shame of whiteness.

Some Woke people thought that an English queen married to Henry the Eighth should not be white, despite historians saying she was white. They made a movie about her and cast a black woman as the queen. It was a strange thing to do, and Ross thought it was wrong. The movie flopped. Enough people agreed that messing with history in such a way wasn't right.

It was all so bewildering to Ross when academics also said that the colour of one's skin doesn't matter. Well, according to one art teacher, white has never been a colour, but a collection of colours, so he concluded, in a truly bizarre way, that it did fit. In any event, there was plenty of history, so replacing one type of person with another was unnecessary. Would anyone in the 21st Century replace people who look like Zulu warriors with people who don't? He didn't think so.

On YouTube, Ross came across these insane academics wanting to decolonise Shakespeare. What next, he wondered, are they going to do it to Charles Dickens as well? And what was so wrong with Shakespeare or Dickens being read in such far-flung places like Australia?

Employed anywhere in Australia, it was best if Ross kept his mouth shut about politics and religion, including social politics, but he wasn't always wise. Sometimes he enjoyed poking the politically correct or Woke bear too much to hear it squeal. He found their nonsense stimulating. The logic was simply beyond them.

Pour the Earl Grey, and let's go nuts, Ross thought one day while playing with a Woke guy on the internet. *I have blue eyes, and my mother has hazel eyes. Does that make me a good guy, a bad guy, or something evil with an angelic mother?* The Woke fellow had no answer to that one.

Ross's family had come out from England, on his father's side, in the late 19th Century and, on his mother's side, after the First World War, and so had nothing to do with how Aborigines were treated in earlier colonial times. Even so, he was continually called upon to share in the guilt of those earlier years. When he questioned immigration, it was always brought up by some self-righteous do-gooding Woke that he, himself, was an immigrant. This, of course, was nonsense since his father and his father's father had both been born in Australia, as had himself. *I am an Australian.* Ross would tell Mr or Ms. Woke, *and you can get stuffed!*

From experience, he knew that feeling sorry for someone doesn't help. It gets them nowhere. Additionally, through the 1975 play The Cake Man by Aboriginal writer Robert J. Merritt, he recognised that various state and federal governments had fostered considerable mistrust by mishandling Aboriginal interests and concerns. Social workers, including those belonging to Christian organisations, had also messed up badly. He had met this writer in college and had found him to be a quiet, reflective man.

Had Aborigines been mistreated for over two hundred years? Yes. Could dwelling on the past help solve present-day issues and lead to a better life for them or anyone? No. Even Ross knew that much!

Ross's time working in the country near Dubbo taught him respect for the working man, whatever their ancestry. He also understood that new families coming into Australia from overseas were not likely to feel any guilt for the past they couldn't have belonged to. Hence, the Aborigines needed to do what they could to find their way in modern Australian society or risk their children being excluded. It wasn't a case of whose society is best, but a question of numbers and how to cope with them. Ross felt knowledge was the key to survival.

He met some army guys one time who suggested Aborigines go back to the bush and live the way they had always lived, and without the white man's further interference. He thought this would be an all-right answer if only new suburbs weren't being developed, resulting in fewer and fewer bushland for them to inhabit.

Ross could understand why Aborigines were not keen on the song *Advance Australia Fair*. It was the national anthem and gave the impression that all Australians were new to Australia, and that didn't fit in with what they understood about their ancestry. Even so, it was where Australia was headed, a conglomeration of a vast number of people from various origins, and that was not going to change, at least not in Ross's lifetime.

Australia was relatively new in terms of federation, which occurred in 1901. Women who were white gained the right to vote in 1902. Decades later, everyone classified as an adult was granted the right to vote. But who to vote for? There was a fine for not voting, so everyone who had to vote did so. Sometimes, Ross felt tossing a coin to decide was the best way to go.

From what Ross could gather, the world was becoming overcrowded, but the significant religions continued pushing for more offspring. The Church and the office, through the system, may have put Ross's sex life on hold, but in this, he understood he was unique. He imagined it had been done to him because the world was in such a state, but he understood he could be wrong there. Stripping one man of fatherhood doesn't accomplish much at all. Later, in old age, Ross was to discover others who had also been made into loners. Even so, he gathered they were small in number, so their forced celibacy could accomplish nothing.

He could see that there would not be enough diseases to cope with the worldwide population increases in the future. Modern warfare, since the First World War, has caused too much damage to cities and towns to be of much use. Many people would naturally diminish through battles, but, unfortunately, the land would suffer and be less useful to anyone who survived. His callous understanding and view of all of this, he put down to his time alone and how he got there. He suspected that his outlook would have been different if he had been put in the position of helping to raise a family of his own. You can't cut someone off from everyday life and not expect, at times, their blood to run cold.

How was he supposed to feel about large families when he felt he had been denied being a husband and a father? Would he have been a good husband or father? He honestly didn't know. He suspected no one knew such things until they were in those positions.

He could do nothing about humanity if it were headed to its destruction. If the end came, he suspected it wouldn't happen in his lifetime or even that of his nieces, though it was possible it would impact their offspring. Scientists are always looking for new and better ways to feed people and eliminate insects that feed upon crops. He had to allow for their success in such ventures.

He remembered a documentary he once saw about DDT. When it first came out, it was described as a modern miracle. It effectively killed insects, including mosquitoes, which carried diseases that affected hundreds, if not thousands, of people. During World War II, it was used in its powder form on American soldiers and Italian civilians to get rid of a lice plague. For generations, it was the favoured insecticide in the USA and elsewhere.

Then, in the 1970s, naturalists made some disturbing findings. First, it was the bald eagles. They were laying eggs that their chicks broke out of too soon. It was then discovered that small mammals were experiencing difficulties with reproduction. Eventually, humans exposed to DDT were examined, and it was revealed that their nervous systems and reproductive abilities were also affected. DDT was banned in the USA and elsewhere, but as far as Ross knew, it was still being used in some countries where people regarded it as the most effective insect killer.

Ross was occasionally told by his sister, Kate, that change was part of life and nothing could remain the same forever. Even so, he objected strongly to those who would censor *The Great Gatsby* or *Tender is the Night* by F. Scott Fitzgerald. He also had a beef with those who would attack *Adventures of Huckleberry Finn* by Mark Twain or *To Kill a Mockingbird* by Harper Lee. Some college and university students were overly sensitive and had gone to great lengths to overlook the importance of such works, instead concentrating on real or imagined faults they could find in the name of diversity.

How come those who demand tolerance are the most intolerant of individuals? For Ross, it was a puzzle. He tried not to be one of them or have much to do with them except to poke fun at their craziness.

When he got into it, he found birding more to his liking than messing about with either political correctness or woke, even if he did enjoy shit-stirring the nutters. Birds made more sense than most people. They were about family as much as getting food and shelter. Still, birds that had been isolated could be overly protective or, if their social needs were not met, go insane.

One magpie per suburb might get agro during spring, with nesting going on, but they were all right for the rest of the year. Nothing changes for the birds unless it comes from humans. When people are involved, some birds cope better than others. In Ross's old age, terns still hunted for food along the south coast beaches, skirting the water, and Oystercatchers scavenged on the sands and rocks, sometimes with success.

CHAPTER TWENTY-TWO

Why Should He Care?

The system frowned upon caring. If it could, it would remove compassion and passion. Blandness was its reward to its followers. Fear of the other, whoever the other might be, was also present.

Growing up, Ross Martin was okay with giving to charity as long as the money went where it was supposed to go. His parents were not wealthy, but his dad did have steady employment. They could afford to go on holiday once a year in May. Never in December because December was a busy time for his dad's workplace.

When Ross was working for the railways, he came upon a fellow in his twenties who had been newly hired and was overjoyed at having a permanent job. "I can think about owning my own home," he told Ross. "I can ask my girlfriend to marry me. All because I am now off the dole!" The fellow was grinning from ear to ear. Was this fellow going to be a slacker? Not likely. He had been given his chance and told Ross there was no way he would muff it. Ross admitted he was happy for the fellow. *This is how it should be*, he thought.

Ross hesitated to help others once he was classified as retired. He imagined aiding the kind of thugs who mucked up in class in high school. No doubt some of them had deservedly fallen on hard times. Am I really that petty? He wondered. Should what some people did in high school follow them for the rest of their lives? Who knows? Maybe some of those thugs had straightened themselves out over the years.

When his lady love volunteered to collect bottles for flood relief one year, Ross felt he had to do something, so he joined her, not wanting to let her down. He told her, though, that he would never do anything for a religion, primarily not raise funds to send Bibles to wherever.

Back in the 1960s, he was told that bringing the word of God to Indigenous Australians living in the outback and New Guinea natives living in the hills of New Guinea was a good thing. He was too young back then to question whether this was true. As it turned out, not everyone connected to the various aspects of Christianity had acted kindly. Stories of abuse came out in the late 20th and early 21st Centuries, and a sizeable part of it dates back to the 1960s. Did this label all of Christianity as bad? No. However, it did highlight that not everyone who calls themselves a Christian can be trusted.

When Ross was young, a Christian program aired every Sunday morning in the USA. This giant dome of a building was all steel and see-through glass. Outside was a car park where the people in their cars could hook up speakers as if they were in a drive-in. On one occasion, it got weird when the preacher inside was selling holy water from France. There was singing, dancing and a great deal of praising the lord. It was the big show that didn't impress Ross's family, including himself, and drove him further away from ever wanting to take Christianity seriously.

Ross found it easy to care for his fellow workers on the railways. It was sometimes hours standing around on an open platform in all sorts of weather. If it was cold, you froze; if it was hot, you sweated. Telling jokes to pass the time between trains going to and coming from the station was the way to go. There were stories about life outside of timetables and the number of people getting off and on trains. Making friends with the station staff who had to be there wasn't hard.

Ross enjoyed his first week in college, and it showed. Even though he felt behind the times and was too old to be so young, he got along fine with most students and tutors. He thought his tutor for film study was a tad too la-de-da, but was impressed when, one day, the fellow cracked a bullwhip and mentioned he had been raised on a farm. He recalled marvelling at his history professor's collection of medieval knight miniatures, which rested on his table in his study next to his computer. They were the type of knights Ross had collected as a boy. He did not, however, mention this to the professor. Now, in his declining years, he wished he had. He was sure the professor would not have been offended but instead amused.

In theatre arts, Ross was never cast in the leading male role. He did, however, have some lively roles in a production of *The Caucasian Chalk Circle*. He remembered what it was like putting on and taking off moustaches and beards. Sometimes, the glue would not hold, and he had to do his best to prevent his beard or moustache from falling off. One role of the seven called for him to have a pot belly, which he achieved via a pillow. It was then he came to realise it was easier for a thin person to play a fat man than for a fat man to play a thin fellow. He wondered what it would have been like to play Shakespeare's Falstaff, but never got the chance. Back then, in college, he recalled, he was indeed thin. Then, ten years of office work led to him gaining weight.

He remembered one day walking into a pub with flowers in hand and getting funny looks. However, he became a fine fellow when he asked the bartender for a couple of bottles of champagne. The barflies then wished him good luck. In truth, the flowers were for the young women actors in a play he participated in, and the champagne was for the entire cast. He wished both flowers and champagne were for one young woman.

Years later, after graduating from college, he could write for the theatre and develop his comedic sense, thanks partly to his college training. He came to care a lot about live theatre, even if he was never likely to play the hero in one of his plays.

He once *saw Cyrano de Bergerac* at the Sydney Opera House. It was done so well that it was memorable, and the swordsmanship was first-class. He wished he could be that good with a sword.

Ross cared about his sister, Kate, and did what he could to make her smile. He remembered one day in the summer when he was asked to dinner at her place. He turned up with a giant watermelon, which he managed to sneak past her and put in her fridge. After the meal, he asked her for a slice of watermelon for dessert. She told him she didn't have any watermelon. He pretended to be offended, saying it was so sad that she was unwilling to share her watermelon. Then her children cracked up laughing, and she said: "There is watermelon!" in a grumpy voice, acknowledging the trick before smiling broadly. This elicited more laughs from her kids. Everyone then had a slice.

On another occasion, he got one of Kate's girls a couple of *Buffy the Vampire Slayer* comics and, at Christmas, a *Buffy* novel. One Easter, one of her children received a moneybox shaped like a coffin. It was one in which you put the coin in the slot and then watched a skeletal hand grab it and place it in the coffin.

Kate introduced Ross to the Harry Potter novels, which he enjoyed. Then, there were the Harry Potter movies, which he watched with Kate and her kids.

Ross's brother-in-law got him out of a tight spot. It was when he lived in the same house with a woman whose kid wouldn't let him watch TV or work on his computer. Even cooking and washing up were too much of a chore in that household. He hated conversations dealing with how hot the water was for washing up.

Before the rescue, getting drunk could ease the pain of paying rent, but it also meant being unable to do the things that made Ross happy. If he had stuck with that woman and her son, he might well have become an alcoholic since there seemed little else to do other than drink away his sorrows. Living in a room where he only got to drink and sleep seemed such a pitiful way to live, and something he wouldn't want to impose on anyone.

Ross and Glenda indulged in beer or champagne only on rare occasions in retirement. They were not heavy whisky drinkers. It had been years since Ross felt the need to get drunk to be social or push away misfortune. Ninety per cent of the time, Ross and Glenda preferred coffee with biscuits while sitting on their porch, watching the sun go down.

CHAPTER TWENTY-THREE

The World Through a Lens!

Photography took Ross Martin out of himself and made him more open to others, provided he took photos of buildings and wildlife, rather than humans. The system was definitely against him taking pictures of people. It had to do with invasion of privacy; he could understand why that would be bad.

Even so, this Italian actress took still photos of Rome. They were black and white, and it was the 1970s. Many of them were just people being themselves without posing for the camera. He believed she got away with it and was able to put them in a book because she was a woman and she was famous.

In old age, Glenda Evens was okay with him taking photos of her, and he took comfort in this. It was evidence that he had truly beaten the system or had it beaten for him.

Ross couldn't remember exactly when he began taking photos. It must have been around ten because he still had a handful of snaps from that time. He was given a Polaroid for Christmas. Before that, he had a camera, but the photos from it were no longer in existence by the time he was in his teens.

When he went to the United States at fourteen, he was given a camera for the trip. He found the cost of the film he bought differed from place to place, with Hawaii being the most expensive. He recalled purchasing a comic book in Honolulu that was more costly there than it would have been in Sydney, Australia.

He travelled from Sydney to San Francisco, then to New York and New Orleans. This was indeed a long trip!

San Francisco was grand. The TV show *The Streets of San Francisco* had been on before he left on this journey, so he knew what to expect and wasn't disappointed. There were a lot of ups and downs in this particularly hilly city. The cable cars were something to be seen and to ride in. He recalled a scene out of Bogart's *The Big Sleep* that had one of those cable cars.

He visited the United Nations building in New York, but didn't think much of it. It was too modern-looking. Later, he would compare the United Nations with the League of Nations and conclude that neither could keep the peace. There would always be war. With the United Nations, because of the atomic bomb and then the nuclear missile, there had to be little wars only. Even so, people were maimed and killed in such conflicts. By the early 21st Century, there was the renewed possibility of conflict in Europe that covered more than two countries.

Ross would have loved to have visited Marvel Comics when he was young, but that was out of the question. It wasn't on his guide's schedule, and he knew he'd get into trouble if he went off alone. Possibly his only chance to meet Stan Lee, Jack Kirby and Gene Colan, and he had to miss out.

In New Orleans, he was shown Australia House, where newspapers and magazines from Australia could be picked up. He visited Bourbon

Street, where artists were painting away. He would have liked to have entered one of the drinking establishments to listen to some jazz, but he was too young. One day, he travelled on the Mississippi and found the water brown with filth. A decade later, he read about how the Mississippi had been cleaned up.

On this trip, he spent a day at Disneyland, marvelling at Future World and the concept of the perfect American town. Later, this town reminds him of an episode of *The Twilight Zone*, in which a man is drawn to such a town because of his desire to escape from hectic modern life. In that place, some kids go fishing and catch fish, while adults pass the time of day with them, and there are no hassles, no pushing for a deadline. It was also the kind of town left to viewers by the fictional girl *Pollyanna*, played by Haley Mills, at the end of the Disney movie that carried her name.

Decades later, there was much criticism over Walt Disney's views on the USA and how he seemed to exclude certain ethnic groups. In truth, though, Ross understood the man could not cover everything that made the USA the USA. That was not possible for anyone. What's more, his presentation was generally not based on solid reality. There were, however, early cartoons that could be considered racist.

In a documentary released in the 21st Century, which Ross viewed, it was noted that Walt Disney had reinvented not only himself but also the town he had come from, turning it into something close to that marvellous turn of the century place (1900 to 1901) in that episode of *The Twilight Zone* and that town at the end of the *Pollyanna* movie.

Ross went to Florida and visited Walt Disney World. There, he found the monorail excellent. He thought it was good of Walt to have set aside wilderness so folks wanting to explore the great outdoors could do so.

Walt Disney Studios experimented with music and animation while Walt was alive. Half a dozen of these animations happened to be brilliant. South American music was put onto these three energetic birds, which Ross liked.

Ross understood that underwater photography took off in the 1950s. It was a case of having better cameras for the job and improved scuba gear. There was talk of Bill Everett's Sub-Mariner becoming a live-action TV show. Unfortunately, this never eventuated.

Then, there was filming skydivers with the large and heavy cinematographer cameras used in the 1960s. He thought the guys who filmed the TV show *Ripcord* had to be all guts, crazy, or both.

Ross was always tempted to laugh at people who would tell him the camera doesn't lie. Even in the early years of cinema, porkies were to be had, which mystified and entertained cinema-goers. He remembered seeing one of the earliest tricks. A magician was filmed waving his magic wand. Then, the scene was filmed both without the magician and with the magician present. Put all three segments together, and the magician disappears and reappears. Cinema magic!

Also, photographs and film footage could be colourised from the early days onward, producing special effects. Black-and-white became red, brown, blue, or purple. Then there was spot colouring, where only a tiny part of a photo or a film was coloured, and the rest stayed black-and-white. This was done with the film *Schindler's List* (1993), in which there are two scenes where a little girl's coat is shown in red, and the rest is black-and-white.

From the 1990s onward, he recognised that it was possible to manipulate digital images using a computer. He didn't like to do it with his photos. There was an ad in which a photographer turned a beach scene pink. He didn't care for that at all. He thought it looked tacky. What's so wrong with sand being yellow, anyway?

Wildlife photography for Ross began with shots of a mouse he took. The little creature was darting this way and that in a railway tunnel close to peak hour, trying not to be stepped on by commuters. The mouse came out as a grey blur. It was a start. He knew that with better equipment, he could get better photos.

The following year, he received a more sophisticated camera for his birthday and focused on capturing photos of lizards, including water dragons and blue tongues. Getting bird photos also became his passion, and it would last for the rest of his life. He would recall being growled at by a young kookaburra and capturing the moment on film. On another occasion, he photographed sulphur-crested cockatoos playing on a wire. They were like children.

CHAPTER TWENTY-FOUR

Science

By the 1990s, the notion that the world was becoming too crowded had vanished, and the idea that it would become uninhabitable also dissipated. Ross didn't understand why. New suburbs continued to be created in NSW, Australia, due to the economic need to attract more migrants from countries experiencing overpopulation. Hence, overpopulation was still a reality even if most Western-style academics no longer believed in it.

For decades, science fiction magazines have featured stories of death rays capable of destroying cities from a platform in outer space or on the moon. When the Russians sent up a probe capable of circling the Earth, alarm bells sounded in the USA, resulting in a race between the Russians and the Americans to the moon.

1969 the United States achieved a significant milestone by landing men on the moon. Ross saw Armstrong place his foot upon moon soil from the comfort of his home via his family's television set. It was in black and white, but that didn't matter. He envisioned a landing on Mars in, say, a decade or two's time. That never happened.

Ross had diagrams of the first module to land people on the moon. It was spindly. It had to be since it couldn't be too heavy. Earlier models were rejected because of weight issues. It looked like one of those water spiders that glide over ponds, only much larger. Ross knew such a module couldn't land people successfully on Mars. The moon was okay because of its lack of gravity and atmosphere. Mars had more gravity plus a possibly poisonous atmosphere.

In the Bond movies, right up to the 1980s, the threat of terror from space, often together with the heating up of the Cold War, seemed a possibility. There was *You Only Live Twice* (1969), *Diamonds Are Forever* (1971) and *Moonraker* (1979).

When the Cold War between Russia and the USA ended, so did the space race. The American military dropped interest in outer space, so landing future men on the moon and creating a habitat for them became a low priority. Also, landing a man on Mars and setting up a crewed station there was unimportant.

In the early 21st century, China's interest in outer space was high. The American comedy *Space Force* (2020) proposed that China might dominate in a future space race.

Ross recalled how people with a scientific mind had historically had problems with the Catholic Church. In the 16th Century, Galileo Galilei wasn't the only one who saw, through a telescope, craters on the moon. However, he got into trouble for revealing this and other natural wonders. The Church leaders of the day envisioned the moon as a heavenly body; to them, it was perfect, like a precious pearl, and they would not have it any other way. Church leaders also believed that the sun and all the stars revolved around the Earth, proclaiming man's importance in the universe. Over time, the Church had to accept this as being wrong.

Ross came across a talk on the internet about a black library within the Vatican, where banned books and manuscripts were kept. Early scientific discoveries may still be found in this library, locked away.

The Southern Cross was important to Ross. It could only be seen at night in the southern hemisphere. It is on the Australian and New

Zealand flags. The cross comprises five stars. He remembered a hiking trip with his dad, where they climbed a hill, and his dad showed him the stars.

Some unintelligent people at university said that because the Southern Cross could be seen in other locations in the southern hemisphere, it wasn't all that unique to Australia and, therefore, could be brushed aside as symbolic of the nation. Ross strongly disagreed. It was there in the night sky, and that's what counted. Was it politically correct or purely woke to undermine one's respect for one's country or even the desire to belong to a nation? He thought it was both. Ross understood his distant ancestors would have seen different night stars.

Optimism was prevalent in the 1960s, as evidenced by American shows such as *Lost in Space* and *Star Trek*. In the 1990s, Ross remembered buying fistfuls of *Star Trek* novels to take north on holiday and thoroughly enjoying them.

Back in the 1970s, Ross collected semi-precious stones. He considered going to Broken Hill to search for opals. He wondered what it would be like to be on the moon, looking for rocks that could tell something unknown about the moon and possibly the Earth.

He had it in his head to become a jeweller one day. Someone who could polish up agates and cut and polish diamonds. This dream, however, was knocked on the head when he discovered that most cutting and polishing machines were made for right-handed people, and it would cost too much for someone in the trade to have a left-handed apprentice needing left-handed machines.

In a primary school in the 1960s, Ross read books about man's relationship with his environment and other creatures. It was touted that humans were the great tool makers, which set them apart from other beings. Meanwhile, while studying chimpanzees in the wild, Jane Goodall was blowing that belief out of the water. Chimpanzees also make tools. They remove leaves from twigs to put these twigs in the termite nests to get termites to eat.

Others have also discovered that orangutans use large leaves as umbrellas when it rains, and mountain gorillas create comfortable beds for themselves out of plant matter. It was also noted that mountain gorillas are social creatures that protect their young. Of course, it took Ross until the 1970s to dismiss what he had learned in primary school and change his thinking.

So, if man isn't the only tool maker (and let's include women), what makes him a cut above the rest? Scientific studies Ross came across in college strongly suggested it was communication. That's how you go from a 19th-century computer only capable of working out horse race results if fed the correct information to machines capable of dealing with the mysteries of outer space.

A Trip to Bali

Ross Martin knew it could be enlightening to see his society from the perspective of someone outside it. Hence, he saw a trip overseas as a way of understanding the system he was under and himself.

Was there much to learn from people living elsewhere? He thought so. In any case, it was a way of experiencing something new he could think about and write about. Were there other systems? He thought there might be, and in this, he was right.

While working in the office, Ross saved enough money for an overseas trip. He chose Bali. He took along his sister, Kate. He felt free of the system there but had no idea what to do with such freedom. This was long before the Bali bombings.

He remembered spending a few days in Ubud in the hills. Where he stayed, there were individual huts with thatched roofs. At night, geckos would inhabit the thatch, so you had a thousand eyes looking down while you slept. Lizard tongues reduced the size of the local insect population. Years later, Ross wished he had gotten a few shots of those geckos with his camera, but he hadn't thought of it then.

Ross found that Balinese coins were lighter and less valuable than Australian money. This meant that Australian money in Indonesia went a long way.

Breakfast was either a fruit salad or bananas on pancakes. Both Ross and Kate opted for bananas on pancakes. The orange juice served with the meal was always fresh.

At night, rice wine was served with a not-too-spicy meal. The wine had a sweet taste, and being alcoholic, it was best only to have a couple of glasses.

While Ross was there, he met a young woman who was half-Chinese and half-white Australian. She was with her father and was rather shy. A German also visited the area yearly to take on the local chess champion. It was a friendly match.

Music was played after dark, and Ross could get some of it taped. It was lively, and the instruments played seemed unique to the place. Only what passed for a flute was recognisable.

One day, a group of Japanese tourists stopped by where Ross and Kate were staying. The Japanese were in their little group and seemed oblivious to anyone nearby. The following day, Ross saw them in the marketplace in the centre of Ubud, all crowded together, taking the same photos of the same things. He wondered if they were frightened to leave their group and examine Bali alone. *Hello! I can be friendly*, Ross thought upon watching them. He also thought they might not understand English and couldn't communicate with him even if they wanted to.

On the outskirts of Ubud, there was an artist's studio. The artist was an Englishman who had spent over a decade in Bali, enjoying the local, laid-back lifestyle. His paintings consisted of many dots on the canvas, creating recognisable pictures.

Ross was not impressed with a group calling itself the New Artists. Perhaps tourists purchased their paintings to bring back something from Bali that could be a valuable future investment. Ross and Kate doubted that anything these guys churned out would make money in the future, but they also agreed they could be wrong.

One day, Ross and Kate follow a dirt road to a village. The people were friendly there, but a young woman breastfeeding a baby was startled by their appearance and went into hiding. Ross wondered why. Months later, when a white woman from New South Wales was caught in Indonesia and jailed for breastfeeding her child out in the open, it all became clear. It made the newspapers.

Ross then realised he could have reported the woman he had seen with her child to the local authorities and gotten her into trouble. He or Kate would not ever do this, but that poor young woman was not to know this. Was this taboo all about making the visiting Christians happy? Ross thought this might be the case; then it occurred to him it could be a Muslim thing, even though most people living in Bali were not of the Muslim faith but of the Hindu faith. Still, there were millions of Muslims elsewhere in Indonesia, so this law might well have had something to do with them. Ross found he hated prudish behaviour generated by fear. He didn't, of course, hate the woman who had every reason to be afraid. He could see a different version of the system he was familiar with at work.

They were invited to a cock fight and were not impressed at seeing birds injured and even killed for no good reason.

They took the bus to Denpasar. It was a rough journey, and Ross and Kate were almost overwhelmed by the potent smell of the red bulbs the local women were chewing. They found Denpasar a busy place. They couldn't get a bus to take them back, so they ended up forking out for a taxi.

Glenda Evens also visited Bali, but this was before she had met Ross. She had adventures, including seeing a stick puppet play and meeting puppeteers from the Rocks in Sydney. She bought three paintings and a scarf at Denpasar. She was not impressed by whatever the men she came across were smoking. It made her feel sick. At one stage, she was offered magic mushrooms, but she declined. She wasn't sure if they were illegal in Bali and didn't want to take her chances.

Years later, she read about undercover police in Indonesia offering drugs to tourists to entrap them and have them jailed. There were also these stupid young men from Australia facing execution for drug trafficking. It was beyond her or Ross as to why anyone would do it if getting caught meant a death sentence.

CHAPTER TWENTY-SIX

Reality

Ross Martin once told his sister and brother-in-law that if you want reality, you should open your front door and go outside. The so-called reality shows of the late 20th and early 21st Centuries were simple-minded garbage. Television networks created programs as cheaply as possible, and young people lapped them up like good little puppies. The System revelled in these television shows.

Reality shows have occurred before and will likely continue to happen. It seemed easy enough to start a trend and promote it as sparklingly new, even though it had been around since the early days of television. Blow the dust away, and you'll be right. Was this the system in action? Ross thought so.

When did so-called reality television start? Ross recalled a documentary about a television show in Australia where a dozen people are taken off the street and made into a jury for a fake trial. The accused, of course, is an actor, as are the phony judiciary members. Would the accused be acquitted or not? Stay tuned after this series of commercials to find out!

In the 1960s, American wrestling on television could entertain a ten-year-old Ross Martin, but it was too staged to be much of a draw for a slightly older viewer. All the bluster at the beginning of these matches was annoying. Did the wrestlers hate each other? No. So why say it's a grudge match when it's just acting? Do people get hurt with this wrestling? Surprisingly enough, it did happen. Sometimes, miscalculation results in injury. This gave the whole thing a sense of being fair dinkum it didn't deserve.

Ross remembered the American show *Candid Camera*, popular among adolescents in 1960s Australia. It had supposedly ordinary Americans being tricked in one way or another by actors in the show. In the 21ˢᵗ Century, an American show called Punk'd was just another go at doing the old *Candid Camera* bit. All dull television if you are older than ten and have active brain cells.

It isn't a tremendous leap from *Candid Camera* and *Punk'd* to *Big Brother*, the show with many incarnations from the late 20th Century in Australia and the UK onwards. It involves putting various people in a house, having them play games, and filming the results. Over time, the games became increasingly elaborate and took on a circus-like atmosphere. Also, it came down to what people should be put together. Could such shows be livened up with folk hostile to one another or those who got along well? How dangerous can the games be, or perhaps they are humiliating?

In any form, just the commercials for *Big Brother* were enough to send Ross out of the room and, on a dozen occasions, out of the house. He didn't care about these people getting so many minutes of undeserved fame. They didn't represent him, nor, if he kept his mind ticking continually over, could they ever do so. They were not his heroes, nor would they ever be. He considered them the lowest of the low because they accepted airtime they didn't deserve.

Ross had read *1984*, so he knew where the reference to *Big Brother* had come from. He feared that, in the future, no one would bother to read the novel.

To him, this so-called reality was dumbing down the viewer to an unacceptable level. What else was there on offer? He found it mind-numbingly sad when a twenty-something dropout tried to get intellectual on camera. She failed miserably because she had nothing to say worth listening to. He suspected young children watching might think otherwise.

He did recall television shows made in Australia in the 1970s that were aimed quite successfully at adolescents without much going for them other than the occasional nude scene. Shows such as *Number 96* and *The Box*. He also recalled a television show called *Alvin Purple* that the censors butchered, which couldn't be displayed at any length on television. It seemed to mark the end of nudity on Australian television, at least for a while.

Ross wrote plays that were staged, satirising Big Brother and other shows that became known as reality shows. His hatred for such shows fuelled, for a time, his creativity. He wanted television to tell him something through scripts and directors. He figured that if the television networks could get away with it, they would have a woman on a stool chatting about her day and nothing more. He couldn't think of anything cheaper than that, and if it could grab an audience, he knew they'd do it.

Penelope went along to see one of his send-ups of so-called reality and was impressed. He and Penelope were surprised to discover that not all the actors he had in his play were against so-called reality. All, though, thought the send-ups a great idea.

After Big Brother's success, the so-called reality spread like cancer. There were shows about people who collected too much stuff and had to have someone help them clean up their homes. There were cooking contests in which the drama of one, captured in an ad, had a contestant accidentally drop a cake. Melodrama was made from that! It was enough to turn Ross off learning to cook anything but basic meals.

Ross suspected he shouldn't have been too down on the music shows that came out of so-called reality since there had always been variety shows on television going back to *Bandstand* in the 1960s. Still, it was the reality packaging he hated most. "But how was new talent in the music field supposed to get out there, in front of a national audience, without there being a music-based reality show?" His sister, Kate, asked him one day. He didn't have an answer for that, though he did think you could still have variety without the reality element.

There were also dancing contests that turned Ross off dancing for a while. He admired such skill in police shows such as *New Tricks*, but not in those dance contests. It was reported that there were stars in such a contest, but he didn't think they were stars. Stars to him had nearly disappeared, thanks to fewer actual television shows with scripts and more of this reality nonsense. Then he decided to go in for a ballroom dance anyway, despite the so-called reality dancing. If he hadn't, he might never have met Glenda Evens. He wasn't fit enough for anything South American but was fine for a lively fox trot. Other women danced with Ross, but only Glenda did he end up dating. Going out with her just seemed so natural. He was surprised at how easy it was initially to ask her to be with him outside the dance hall.

Weddings were not to be spared. What happens when couples marry at first sight? Do they get along? What can go wrong? What happens when the make-up comes off, and the husband sees the bride first thing in the morning? Who cares? That was Ross's answer, but there were viewers in the UK and Australia who had to find out about such things in these reality shows.

Reality television, if nothing else, got Ross out of the house more and more. His collection of DVDs and paperbacks also grew. Even so, he had to put up with reality ads while viewing the news in the evening. He grumbled over them. He stopped doing so, however, when he came to live with his lady love. He felt such grumbling was as unfair on her as the ads were on him.

By the beginning of the 21st Century, there were more science fiction shows on television to enjoy, which took the sting out of so-called reality. He especially liked the television show *Westworld*. Birding also helped, as did photography in general. The great outdoors beckoned, and he more and more answered that call.

To Hell with the Rest of the World

To Ross Martin, honeymoons were about a couple declaring their love for each other and saying to hell with the rest of the world. This generally took place somewhere they had never been before and away from as many people they knew as possible. Then it was back to friends, family, and that part of society no longer against their happiness. The system was defeated.

When he was young, he listened to The Seekers. The song that grabbed his attention was A World of Our Own. As he grew up, he understood how the lyrics identified what was wrong with society and how couples had to fight to be together.

There was once a playwright who said that Hell was other people. The playwright was Jean-Paul Sartre, and the play was *No Exit*. Ross constantly amended this, in his thoughts, to "Hell is other people," as pushed by the system.

Was this how it was always supposed to be? He wondered. He had this notion when his sister, Kate, returned from her honeymoon. He had not wished her or her husband any ill will, but could understand their desire to escape from everything and be alone. There was no chance then of anyone, for a brief time, dragging them down into Sartre's version of the devil's region.

Ross didn't quite have that honeymoon period with Glenda, but he did have something similar. Once they had found a new home with a beach nearby, they were alone for a while, being good company for one another. Why did most of the world even care if Ross and his lady were happy?

Over the years, Ross had felt betrayed by both religion and custom. The system's many tendrils were forever trapping or trying to trap him. What kind of a world did the religious want for him and themselves? Why was sadness a more customary and safer state to avoid the system than joy? The answer was simple. No one can pull you down when you are already down, but if you're up, there is a definite way the system can use against you.

The idea that if you do what you are told in this life, you will do well in the next one was a puzzle. How can that be, and why should it be? Throughout the ages, he imagined all these peasants thinking that once they died, they'd get everything they could want in Heaven. He thought it would be great if that were true, but how could it possibly be so?

Was reincarnation real? Had he been born before, and were there still traces of his past? This would explain Ross's brother, Ian's, success with Susan, the horrid woman he married. His past life had somehow pointed him in the best direction. In other words, what can be taken as instinctual are lessons learnt from an earlier life. So, where did this leave Ross? He figured he must have once been a monk and knew nothing of consequence back then, particularly regarding relationships with women.

As a child, Ross tended to look up to adults in a way foreign to his brother Ian. He didn't question those in charge, such as teachers, until he was in college. Maybe Ian had been a rogue in a past life and still had that about him.

Was the belief in reincarnation anti-Christian? No, though the Catholic Church authorities banned it. The idea of being given many chances to get life right appealed to Ross. It did not appeal to Glenda, who felt one go at life on Earth was more than enough for anyone.

What Ross couldn't understand was a God who didn't want him to be happy in the present. Could such a being exist, or was it a product, a construct, of the system? Did someone make up a God to keep the likes of Ross in line and thus forever in their clutches? Decades before he met Glenda, there were stupid, though well-meaning, religious people in his life. However, he didn't know how foolish or religious they were then.

Over the years, he had thought he might be a spiritual person, but not at the expense of his body's needs and wants. He was flesh and blood.

Ross thought one day, while sitting on a pew and paying attention to a Methodist preacher in a nice suit, that if the Church could not help me with flesh and blood matters, then how could it do anything for my soul if I do have one?

He remembered going to this hall with his dad and other parents and kids for an event put on by a dozen Church groups to help put a stop to misinformation about sex that was being passed around in various playgrounds. He was about nine or ten and mystified by this gathering and its reason. As far as he knew, sex and religion had nothing to do with one another. This was an example of early sex education, and, for Ross and other boys and the girls that were there, it was both embarrassing and useless.

The mechanics of sex were discussed in some detail, with drawings, but how men and women got together to make love was left out. What do you say to someone of the opposite sex you want to get to know and be with? Nothing was said about the spark in the eyes that ignites everything, and how it was so essential for a lad to look for that spark in the eyes of a young woman. Life is calling to life as it has done for countless generations.

There was talk about what young boys and girls must not do, which was fair enough. No one wanted girls to get pregnant when they were too young to cope. Nothing was said about what age in the life of a human male or female it was okay to think about copulation. Ross was told it was best not to venture there, even in thought, but he did so anyway, in thought only.

He increasingly understood that life was better than the slim possibility of reward after death. Here, his brother Ian got ahead of him by getting a young woman pregnant (they were in their late teens and early twenties) and later marrying her.

Was religion all about death? It was that way to young Ross, seated in that Methodist church on a Sunday, and also after that abortive sex talk in that windy hall. Life, however, did call to him sometimes, but he had no idea how best to answer.

Ross understood that two thousand or so years ago, a holy man who may have been the son of God had not set things up so that a fellow born in Australia in the 20th Century would miss being a dad. He was unaware of anything in the Bible that pointed to one man being cheated of a wife and offspring and another being granted these precious things.

Did Christianity start as a death cult offshoot of Judaism? Ross understood that some scholars held this view. Over two thousand years later, Christianity wasn't like that, or so he thought. But what was it like? Glenda and his sister, Kate, believed it was full of kindness, but he could never see it that way.

It doesn't take anyone long to realise that no one lives forever. Ross was made aware of this when his grandfather, on his mother's side, passed away. His grandfather had fought in World War One and had been so gravely wounded in France that he should have died there, but did not do so. He returned to Australia with his newly acquired wife and was fit enough to do carpentry work and help raise his family. He crafted toys out of wood and became renowned for his artistic skill. For decades, he carried bits of shrapnel in his lung because it would do too much damage to take it out. Eventually, he had to die, leaving his grown-up offspring with fond memories of him.

Ross was always told to make the most of life while he still had it. In his early years, this meant making the most of the family holiday up north since he hated school and was a loner. He could forever recall one glorious day on the Clarence River while on holiday with his folks. He had a new comic book to read, a fishing rod to fish with, and his family around him. It was sunny but not too hot.

According to Ross, the natural way of existence is that we live on in our children. But what if that isn't so? What if the system gets in the way and, thanks to it, you don't have a wife and offspring? And what did the system and those who supported it gain by dismissing Ross as a human being? The answer he came up with in college made sense to him.

Finding the right woman and all that followed was the ultimate test. He was meant to risk everything for little gain. Rewards were cumulative, and so were punishments for not having a go. He was supposed to venture out into the wild, where sharp claws tore up not flesh but degrees and jobs, and take his chances.

The few risks he took in college, which were taken when drunk, didn't work out. After leaving college, he was determined to find work and hoped for the best. He also wanted the books he would write to be his offspring, to live on after death. His sister, Kate, thought this very strange, but Penelope, his friend from college, understood.

Political correctness was in full swing then, and there was talk of women taking back the night. He had no idea what that meant since he didn't think the night had been taken away from them in the first place.

He took it as another way in which the system could and did keep him down. In his old age, he wondered if women were still fighting to take back the night or if it had ended sometime in the 1990s.

Looking back on history, he figured the Vamps of Europe had secured the night before and after the First World War. They were in seductive black long before the 1960s and 1970s, and those excellent Hammer vampire flicks. Ross once saw a 1915 silent movie featuring a vamp. The star was Theda Bara, who looked dark, sinister, exotic, and magnetic. This was before the advent of censorship in Hollywood movies.

A female vampire scene in the film Dracula (1931) was cut due to censorship. At the time, censors were squeamish about having females in such alluring roles as vampires. Unfortunately, only publicity still exists for that scene, but Ross, having seen them in a classroom at college, had to agree that it was such a pity that the actual film footage could no longer be seen.

In the 1920s, jazz musicians and dancers stirred things up in France, the United States, Canada, and Australia. In the USA, there was a prohibition against drinking alcohol, which, for law enforcement, didn't turn out to be a clever idea. There were speakeasies where people drank in secret, and big money was to be made smuggling alcohol down from Canada.

Still wild, joyous times that made up, in small ways, for the horrors of the First World War couldn't last forever. In 1929, the Wall Street stock market crash profoundly impacted Americans and the rest of the world. Millions of people were impoverished. Prohibition was ended because the American government needed to be able to tax alcohol fully. Then, a second World War had to occur, followed by the Korean War and the Vietnam War. Finally, 9/11 and, after that, little wars that drained Western-style countries financially and cost lives.

For Ross, in his earlier years, the night held a promise that was never fulfilled. Now, as he was getting to the end of his life, he had to wonder what those female disco dancers were now like and what kind of husbands, if any, they had managed to land. Did they even want husbands and children? Did they even think about a future without themselves being present? He did, at given times, think a son or a daughter might have been wonderful—someone to continue after he was gone.

He figured those dancers got whatever they wanted, and he was best to leave it there. If he were to judge them, he didn't have much to go on, and he knew it. He couldn't remember what they looked like, the ones he saw dancing, those he asked for a dance with or the women who danced with him.

He'd never forget dancing with a female PE teacher in high school. And then there was dancing with Penelope, holding her close as if she could mean something to him other than friendship. He now dances on occasion with Glenda Evens. It was something they both enjoyed, and it kept them a couple.

In not remembering the young ladies of the disco, he was lucky. He meant nothing to them and was happy to have them mean zero to him. Maybe they were necessary for someone somewhere, and that, in the end, was fine with him.

Ross's brother, Ian, had two daughters who would be alive well after he was gone. His sister, Kate, also had children. This was so right that he felt, before he met Glenda, like raising a fist to the system, crying his defiance of it for short-changing him. However, one person cannot go up against the system and win. There must be two. If this second person cannot be found, then anything Ross did against this mystical body would be useless. He found his other, his delight, too late for offspring but not too late to defeat the system, this creation of the society he had lived in all his life.

It was through his writing that Ross hoped to live on, so he was dismayed when college and university students, full of themselves, decided to attack literary giants whose works he cared about.

He wondered why Roald Dahl's children's stories, such as *Matilda* and *Fantastic Mr Fox*, had to be censored and words changed to meet Woke demands.

Ross was unsurprised that Woke wanted to do something similar to *Adventures of Huckleberry Finn*. That particular novel by Mark Twain has been criticised for one reason or another since it first saw print. When it first came out, the people in the American South didn't like it because it seemed to be anti-slavery. In the 1980s, some people felt its language was a problem. Recently, this so-called issue with language use resurfaced.

The Great Gatsby, by F. Scott Fitzgerald, was criticised in the 21st century for being perceived as anti-black. In truth, the book did have a racist character who was also a wife-beater and a bully. This relates to the need for novels to have both villains and heroes.

The movie *Pleasantville* (1999) captured past attacks on literature and art. On a wall, there was a painting of the covers of famous novels that had been banned at one time or another.

He thought film and television might be a way of cheating death, but he discovered, through one of his nieces, that this was not to be. She refused to watch anything that was in black and white. This meant half his DVD library meant nothing to her. He wondered what present-day movie and television making would likely mean to future humans—no doubt, they would find a reason to be dismissive. Since twenty per cent of what was being made in the early 21st Century was Woke rubbish, there would be some justification for doing so.

Ross knew enough about science to theorise that any species continually increasing its numbers would be in for a backlash from nature.

Back in the 1980s, there was the threat of AIDS. If nothing else could, the possibility of getting it through casual sex was enough to scare anyone out of being so casual about it. The ad on television, with the Grim Reaper knocking down people with a bowling ball because of this disease, was meant to terrify.

AIDS never went away, but after a while, it could be managed better in the West. New medications were available to sufferers. They could live longer. In African countries, the shortage of medical supplies remains devastating. There was talk about how sex with a virgin would cure AIDS. This was complete nonsense, but some desperate people came to believe it and try it out.

In the 1990s, a variation of swine flu and the threat of mad cow disease were around. Neither was much of a bother to Ross. He got a flu shot to get him through winter every year, and that was that. There always seemed to be something about to mess up a sex life. Still, the brave and the good-looking always managed to find a way.

In the early 21st Century, it was COVID-19. The story was that it came from China, not with love. Was this by accident or design? Ross thought it was an accident. Was it really from China, or was this scuttlebutt? He didn't know. When he first heard about it, he thought it was a joke, but unfortunately, it was a serious and contagious illness.

Ross got his two preventative shots and felt fine. After those injections, Covid-19 was not likely to take his life, but the disease hanging around reduced what he could do while it was affecting the world. Having people carrying it meant wearing a mask when he went out. No one, including himself, wanted to die from it. There was then no possibility of dancing cheek to cheek somewhere with someone. That would have to come later.

Eventually, he had to get a third preventative shot, and so it went on and on for years. To cheer himself up, he bought books and DVDs online. If he was ever to bust out of being a hermit, these were not the years to do it in, but he knew, even then, his time was running out, and he didn't want the system to win its final victory over him by default.

It was a wonder he met Glenda just in time to have two good years with her. There was a third year, but since that was a year with cancer, he felt it didn't count. If those two years were a miracle, it was a good one, and if God had made it happen, then he wasn't so bad after all and should be worshipped. This, however, had nothing to do with any church or religious group. Instead, his thanks and appreciation went out to the great void, the stars and the creator.

CHAPTER TWENTY-EIGHT

Fine! The World Can Enjoy Our Happiness!

Ross Martin discovered it was so easy to be self-indulgent when it came to happiness. He was even self-righteous about it. He needed Glenda Evens and no one else. His sister, Kate, had been good to him, and Penelope was too. They could stay. Others had been anything but kind, and they, standing for the system, remained too much in his thoughts and actions. They could go away. In sending them away, he felt no need to deal with them further.

Soon after dating, Ross and Glenda dropped out of ballroom dancing. For a while, they went to live theatre and bushwalking instead. Neither saw anything wrong with those in their ballroom dance club. Glenda said she wanted to get to know Ross better and that Ross wanted to get to know her better away from others.

Ross knew his greatest revenge against the system was his happiness with Glenda, but he didn't feel like flaunting it, just in case the system had a final card to play—one that would cancel out his happiness or that of the woman he loved. Could it come during a ballroom dance? He didn't think so, but he did remember that dance with Penelope and how she felt sorry for him because his relatives were so shocked to see him with a beautiful woman.

What did he owe anyone who would make loneliness his lot? The answer was nothing. If they were doing it to him, were they also doing it to themselves? He thought this was possible. A self-righteous idiot could do that to themselves and worse. Were there present-day religious freaks beating themselves up daily because they have feelings? Why shouldn't there be present-day Flagellants?

Were there people struggling to escape the system whom he could help? He thought this a possibility. What aid, though, could he offer them?

Helping others wasn't his thing, but he could make it so. Glenda made quilts for Angel Flight to sell. Angel Flight is an organisation that offers free flights to transport people in remote areas to hospitals when they need such a service.

Glenda wanted to open herself and him up to the world. They had a lovely place close to a beach, ideal for entertaining. She told him no one could take away what they had together.

"We decide how we live our lives," she told him. "We're both old enough to make those sorts of decisions."

"But what about…," began Ross.

"But what about nothing?" concluded his lady love. "We're safe! We're okay!"

"But for how long?" he wondered.

"For as long as close to forever as we can manage," she replied.

"Well, that will have to do," he told her, smiling sheepishly.

He resisted at first to this opening up to the world. She told him it was foolish to be cold toward those who would otherwise be their friends. He told her of the days he was in tears over not being close to anyone the way he was with her and how he felt he had been driven down that path of being alone by what he called the system. "If it exists, it has gone now," she told him. "If it comes back, together we can shoo it away!" He sighed and said, "If only that were possible."

In the end, she won, and they branched out together. He had his qualms at first, but he had no regrets in the end. He had family, and she had family, too. It was time they all got together over lunch or dinner. She decided it should be dinner. Both oversaw the meal, and it was a nice start. Weeks later, he introduced Kate and Glenda to his old college friend, Penelope.

Thanks to his sister, Kate, her husband, and their children, plus Penelope, Ross had never been entirely alone, even though it sometimes felt that way. Glenda also had a sister and two brothers, who had their children. The get-togethers with that entire lot made up for the hurt Ross had felt in past years. It was also suitable for Glenda.

"I have won," Ross told her one day, "and it need not be a secret."

"From what you have told me about the system," she replied, "it belongs in the shadows, and so cannot stand the light. While we are in the light, it cannot harm us."

Going back into the light meant rejoining the ballroom dance club. They did so and were both heartily welcomed. None of the other members were against Ross and Glenda being together, nor did anyone feel sorry for anyone else.

Ross Martin firmly believed that only those not promoting the system were entitled to criticise it. He did not consider preachers worthy of this distinction, except for a few. Despite the Methodist preacher who made Sundays less than ideal, Ross would not seek revenge as it was not worth his time or effort. He believed that communists, politically correct, and the lunatic Woke were too involved in the system ever to deserve to be free from it. He also knew that they would not accept help from anyone, including him, to escape from the traps they had set for themselves.

Ross felt that communism, political correctness, and the Woke movement offered no hope. Woke comic books, movies, and television shows were so off-putting that few people cared to indulge in them. Woke had managed to destroy Doctor Who. Ross understood that a significant percentage of those involved in Woke thought they were being heroic rather than dumb. They wanted to change the world without much thought behind their approach.

Do souls exist? Ross always thought so. It seemed to him that he was more than just a body. When he went to sleep on full moon nights, he felt like he drifted, going elsewhere in time and space.

Did souls come in all shapes and sizes? Possibly. He imagined his sister Kate's soul was more prominent than his own because she was more compassionate. Shortly before he met his lady love, she looked after him when he broke his arm. She stood by him after their parents had passed away and urged him to get involved with more people.

Ross was familiar with a man who was always popular with women. Many men in the local area envied him for his way with the opposite sex. From his teenage years, he would enjoy wild weekends engaging in one-night stands and never really paying attention to the movies he went to see at the drive-in. It became clear to him over time that the young women he was with didn't take him seriously. However, his life began to unravel when he finally found someone who did and got married. He turned to alcohol and ended up getting a divorce. Ross suspected the man was only comfortable with short-term flings and didn't know how to handle a long-term, committed relationship. The last time Ross heard about him, he was unemployed, still drinking excessively, and had gained weight. Ross learned that love can be a complicated and delicate thing.

In the second season of the 1970s show *Wonder Woman*, there is a silly song titled *Love Conquers All*, but is it all that ridiculous, the title that is? Love might not be able to defeat the system by itself, though it could have it groggy, on the ropes, and ready for the knockout blow. Ross figured out that much. Glenda helped him do it.

No one deserves to be alone. If God exists, He, She, or It would want humans to be with other humans. If not, then God should be feared. However, when he found Glenda, he knew that God could be kind and not to be feared.

Ross realised he was better off being alone than with the wrong company. He understood that sometimes one must endure an unpleasant situation, such as when he shared a house with someone who disapproved of his computer usage. Although it wasn't the worst thing that could have happened to him, it was still challenging. By the time he met Glenda, he had a silent PC, but it didn't have to be that way. He no longer had to worry about being interrupted when he wanted to write or surf the internet. Additionally, he was no longer constantly lending money to someone who made more than he did. It was a relief to be able to save money.

While studying history, Ross imagined the generations of young men who went to war and never returned. For decades, he believed these men were lucky because the system adored them. Being dead, they were not a bother to anyone. Meanwhile, Ross had survived the Vietnam War, as he was too young to be drafted. However, he had lived in a state of half-deadness. Sometimes, he wondered what it would have been like to have died early with a big grin without suffering a great deal or sin mightily.

Because of his grandfather, the one wounded during the First World War, Ross knew that the hardships of battle didn't always end with peace. American movies had it, from the 1940s up until well into the 1970s, that soldiers survived with either minor injuries or none. The rest were killed outright. However, a trip to a veteran's hospital in Australia in the 1970s showed life not to be that simple. What happened to anyone in armed combat, good and bad, had to do with luck. A small percentage of people managed to go through the most horrific of scenes without a scratch while watching their mates blown to bits.

Ross knew that the American war comics published in the 1960s were about promoting patriotism and less about reality. For instance, a comic book issue of Sergeant Fury and his Howling Commandos depicted a group of American commandos in World War II, France, infiltrating a town full of German soldiers with tanks and screaming at the top of their lungs. Ross knew that, in reality, those commandos would have been obliterated as soon as the enemy was alerted to their presence. However, in the comic book, they had to triumph as the heroes. Ross found it illogical that a commando would blow a bugle before going into action.

Western comics of the 1960s were no better. The protagonist, be it Marvel's The Rawhide Kid or any other character, was not allowed to be depicted killing anyone, even in a fair gunfight. This was primarily due to the Comics Code Authority, which censored American comics and restricted the content that could be illustrated. As a result, the illustrations were limited and predictable, making Western comics lose their charm quickly. Even a ten-year-old could easily figure out what could and could not be shown. As a reader, one could predict what would happen next even before turning the page.

Some American comic books cater to female readers with stories about true love, such as Marvel's "Millie the Model". However, these comics did not sell well as most girls and young women were not interested in reading comic books. On the other hand, Archie Comics, which focused on teenage misadventures, gained a large readership. In contrast, English comic papers, like "Daisy", had a female following, including Ross's sister Kate when she was young.

Throughout his life, Ross had encountered jocks and jockettes starting from primary school. He felt like an outsider because they were passionate about sports, but he wasn't. Although his dad used to play cricket before getting married, he wasn't a jock either. He enjoyed playing sports just for the exercise and camaraderie they offered. Ross initially struggled to accept this and tried to prove himself by participating in various sports, but none worked out. He was still haunted by the thought that his younger brother Ian would have been stronger than he if he hadn't contracted scarlet fever at a young age.

Ross hoped to impress his paternal grandfather with his fishing skills during their vacation up north in May. However, the fish at Iluka, where he usually fished, were not biting that year. The beach's ebb and flow had changed, and excessive trawling resulted in no significant catch for anyone, including his grandfather. Although Ross later realised it didn't matter, he was disappointed that he couldn't prove his worth to his grandfather. However, he was still happy fishing with a rod in his hands. He was skilled at casting and enjoyed doing it, not just to show off. Besides, catching fish depended on factors beyond his control, such as the fish's presence and willingness to bite.

Ross pondered whether anyone deserved the good things in life in his final years. While luck certainly played a role, he believed goodwill was equally important. He concluded that to achieve success, one needed both luck and goodwill. Without them, one had to wait for an opportunity to present itself or engage in various activities and hope for the best. However, with Glenda, he was fortunate enough to have both luck and goodwill on his side. He couldn't imagine living without her. He knew he was being selfish by wishing to pass away first, but he had been through enough hard times without the kind of companion he wanted and needed.

He still felt stung by his aunt's horrid sympathy for him, even though he hadn't seen her in a long time. He realised she might never know about him and Glenda. *And she doesn't deserve to see Glenda and me together, he thought,* on more than one occasion. She could have had more going for her if she had kept her head straight. Could she have become a renowned artist? He doubted that. However, when she did have good looks, she might have faked having artistic talent, and there could have been those who wanted to see the genius in her paintings. Good looks could go a long way when promoting art of every sort. She had been one of the beautiful people for too long to understand the struggles of others, but he still blamed her for getting him wrong.

CHAPTER TWENTY-NINE

Dancing Skeletons

Ross Martin had encountered skeletons in a dozen cultures, including his own. He knew the system used them to frighten people into following their rules. They didn't scare him, though he suspected they had that effect on others.

He was cruising YouTube near Easter, the first year he lived with Glenda, when he came across these cavorting skeletons. They were an early Disney creation. They were lively for creatures without any more substance than black-and-white images on so many cells. They mocked both life and death with horrid grins. He found them amusing. He figured they were for Halloween. He recalled cartoon cells from Disney and elsewhere being for sale at a shop on one of the floors of the Victoria building in Town Hall, Sydney. He marvelled at how much went into the making of each cell to create a motion picture. Was there a cell from these dancing skeletons? He couldn't recall. He remembered there were also framed ads for various products and posters of famous movies.

The gambolling skeletons brought him back to his medieval studies in college and a time in human history when death was mysterious and life was short. Was the system fully operational at the time? He didn't think so, since it didn't have to be that way to be effective. Partially in operation would have been enough. During the poor harvest years followed by the plague years, if someone lived past thirty, they were considered to be doing well. They were doing even better if they hadn't been in a war with injuries that would last a lifetime. Where it existed, medical help was primitive.

It was expected that a boy wouldn't be admitted into the town or village as a member until he turned ten. Death among the very young was high, and it was also high during the 19th Century in the United Kingdom. In terms of survival, girls did better in their early years. The danger for them came later with pregnancy. Unsanitary conditions in some places in the Middle Ages and 19th-century England, combined with a lack of medical knowledge, were the primary causes.

Ross recalled a room in a house he once lived in. The place dates back to the 19th Century. The bedroom ceiling had plaster infants with angel wings. He imagined there had been a sizable number of infant deaths at the time of the plastering.

Ross recalled that dancing skeletons were depicted on doors and in European manuscripts during the Black Death. Many people got the plague, and there was the belief in some quarters during this time to make merry as much as possible lest you die with regrets. If you will become a skeleton anyway, why not make the most of your life while you still have one? Meanwhile, others were trying so hard to get right with God that they were ruining not only their lives but also the lives of others. This was the system in action.

Back when plague could strike at any time, saving one's soul must have been a top priority for thousands of people. Buying indulgences from the Church to save oneself or a loved one from trouble after death seemed an effective way to spend what little savings a person had. Thus, with these indulgencies, one pope could fill his coffers and advance his building projects.

Then, Martin Luther could not see any references to indulgences in the Bible and became a troublemaker. He was also opposed to the Church charging people to view holy relics. In the end, Martin Luther formed his church, which had nothing to do with indulgences and other matters that Luther could not find in the Bible. Was Luther attacking what was then the system? Ross thought that might be the case. In doing so, Ross wondered if Luther wasn't inadvertently creating his version of the system. He got some of his information about Luther from a Lutheran church.

Lust was nothing new, and neither were rule breakers. He understood that people tended to be on the side of those who went against custom and religion and had gotten away with it. Life is more important than death and dancing skeletons. Was Ross such a person in old age with Glenda? He liked to think so, but he knew better. If he had triumphed earlier, yes. Time was a factor in all of this. Lust no longer meant as much to him as it did when he was a twenty-something kid.

Ross wanted to be a believer but kept running into reasons not to believe. In Giovanni Boccaccio's 14th-century collection of stories, *The Decameron*, monks and nuns with sexual appetites indulge in them. In this great work, monks are a bit too comforting to widows. Was there such hypocrisy in the Church back then? Ross gathered this was so, but he didn't know how widespread it was, nor was he likely to find out. Was celibacy a joke back then? He didn't know. He knew that celibacy had started with some pope. Why? Maybe it had to do with the fear of God generated by the knowledge that death could come at any time.

Ross knew that the breaking of celibacy had taken on sinister meaning in the 20th and 21st Centuries, with some priests accused in Ireland, the USA and Australia of the mistreatment of children in their care. Given this, a pope having a mistress didn't seem such a bad thing to Ross. However, how he managed to have a family and remain Pope remains a mystery.

Ross once read of a monastery on a hill, a nunnery on another hill, and an orphanage in the valley between them. Readers were left to draw their conclusions. What happened to these children once they left the orphanage? Perhaps they became nuns and monks.

In the early 21st Century, antisemitism spread throughout Western-style countries such as the UK, the USA and Australia. It had to do with the influx of Muslims into these countries, plus the easy manipulation of college and university students and professors. Somehow, there was a marriage between Muslim extremism and Marxism. Those two beliefs didn't belong together. Even so, they had come across a mutual enemy and were together.

Why peaceful, law-abiding Jews should be targeted was not entirely understood by Ross. He thought that when it came to the Muslim extremists, it had to do with getting good with Allah. With death not so near as in the past, why weren't these extremists capable of reasoning out their actions and simply going for a live-and-let-live way of existence? Maybe in some third-world countries, the ones they came from, death was still too close.

In 2023, Israel was attacked. Did the people of Israel have every right to defend themselves against Hamas terrorism? Ross thought so. He also reasoned that Hamas was responsible for life being unpleasant in Gaza as well as elsewhere. So why did members of the United Nations support Hamas? It was a sign that the United States, the United Kingdom, Israel, and Australia should no longer sponsor the United Nations.

For a long time, Ross had been aware of the four horsemen of the apocalypse, with the Grim Reaper as one of them leading the others on. There was Plague, Famine, and War. Did it matter in what sequence they rode or if they rode together? Ross didn't think so. In medieval times, millions of people were eliminated, and then they were gone. Was the system affiliated with the present-day versions of these horsemen? He thought this might be the case.

Two years with Glenda in defiance of the system was grand, but what followed in the third year was cancer eating away at him. Glenda stuck with him, and he had family, so he tried not to burden any of them too much.

When his time came to die, Ross wanted to dance with those old skeletons and make his last moments on earth merry. He was now with a woman he could genuinely love, which counted for everything.

This is the End, My Friend

Ross Martin lay in bed with tubes sticking out of him. It was how many of the men in his family had died, and he couldn't see why he should be an exception. It had to be better than bleeding to death on a battlefield. It was just his physical self that was packing it in. What would remain of himself once that was done? His soul, perhaps? The system for him was dead, killed off three years ago. Two good years with Glenda and one year with cancer. He wrote about his demise.

Were there bodyless entities wandering the corridors of this hospital? He thought that might be the case, but had no way of knowing while alive.

Will I get to see angels? He wondered. *And if I do, will they be kind to me?* He suspected a preacher of any sort would say yes to both questions, but he didn't want answers from any preacher. He didn't think they were connected to either God or angels.

He took comfort in his defeat of the system and his time with his lady love. She brought him flowers, and he told her how flowers were

meant to ward off illness. "Not much good for a body wearing out," He told her with a smile, "but it's the thought that counts."

He wanted to believe in God, a merciful one who saw him as not such a bad person. He had believers, including Kate, Penelope, and Glenda. He thought believing would be so marvellous, especially that day after he had tripped, fallen, and broken his arm. A nurse who saw him fall helped him to Wollongong Hospital. She probably saved his life. It took months to regain any use of the arm. At that time, he wanted to have faith more than ever before, but it was not to be.

Those years when his television, DVDs, computer, and books provided some relief from his hurt took their toll. He had spent too much time alone, for which he blamed the system and his Christian connection to it.

He continued to believe that if God existed, it would not have been God's intention for Ross to have endured so much loneliness. It was part of the free will clause in the contract that he thought had more to do with Christian groups than any God. Were other religions just as bad? He thought so. He didn't imagine Islam being any better. He thought it might have been worse.

He knew there were well-meaning reasons behind his being alone for so long, but put that firmly down to human rather than superhuman causes and reasoning. Above all else, he didn't want to believe in a cruel God. If God were that inclined, what chance did anyone have for a great afterlife? None he could imagine.

Was God responsible for his getting cancer and becoming a diabetic? No. He thought humans could take all the credit. Cancer, except skin cancer, no doubt came from all the foods that had preservatives and artificial sweeteners added. Diabetes was the result of a sugar addiction that wasn't there when what was sweet was either hard to come by or seasonal. The supermarkets were loaded with items containing sugar.

Glenda, his lady love, didn't understand his reluctance to take religion, any religion, seriously, even when he was in the hospital on his deathbed. Too much taken away, he told her, and no explanation was given as to why he and not somebody else. When pressed, he told her, even if it was only two per cent religion and the rest of his stupidity, why he had been alone, he still couldn't buy into it.

He had been with her for two golden years. The year with cancer is not so golden, but still much better than being alone. It took the sting out of the decades he had lived by himself, but not enough. The best he could do was to ignore the less comfortable past and bask in those two years. But even those less-than-comfortable years had their good moments. He enjoyed working for the railways and made friends while doing so. Thanks to that time, he knew more about the railways and how they ran than most people knew or wanted to know.

The published stories he wrote also helped vindicate his life—if indeed it needed vindication. He kept on writing until he finally landed in the hospital with no hope of recovery.

In those two wondrous years, he and his lady love had travelled together across Australia from Sydney to Darwin to Perth, then down to Tasmania. Even the winters were much better with a companion to share them with. Being close to a beach meant it never got cold when he wasn't travelling. There were fewer birds to photograph in those cooler months, which made spring glorious. The summers were hot, but not unbearably so. He lost weight because of his walks, and so did Glenda.

He divided the great collection of writing and photography he had accumulated between his sister, Kate, Penelope, and Glenda. His DVDs and books would go to whoever wanted them. These were things from him that he could leave behind. He was glad these women got along so well. He didn't expect his writing to last forever, but a decade or so in the right hands would be good. He hated the idea of some future sensitivity editor laying hands on anything he had written.

The Woke nonsense of the early 21st Century had convinced him that nothing could last forever. What eventually happened to Woke showed him that the bad had to change, adopt a different name and persona, to keep going. Someone was always out to profit from someone else's ignorance and arrogance. Some people didn't care how much money they flushed down the toilet so long as they got their views out among the people.

He was surprised at the efforts made to bring the Fantastic Four to the screen and how many people got it wrong. The last attempt had the team run by the Invisible Woman rather than Mr. Fantastic. Moreover, it was decided on a female rather than a male Silver Surfer. Hence, the comics of the Fantastic Four would remain true to what Jack Kirby and Stan Lee had in mind for as long as the publisher decided to continue to make them so. In any case, his collection of the old Fantastic Four comics, which Jack Kirby and Stan Lee were responsible for, would go to someone in the family and hopefully be enjoyed by them.

Ross couldn't be bothered with his past mistakes now that he was near the end. They were useless to anyone, including his sister and Glenda. He suspected the system would continue without him, but he had no advice worth anything for anyone caught up in it. The rules kept changing. What had once kept young men, such as he had been, in place had changed. All he could say to anyone facing the system was to battle on, take your lumps and try to team up with someone who cares. "I should have taken more lumps earlier, " he told his sister. "If I had gotten that over with and learned from the bruises, who knows where I might have ended up?"

There was no one left to fight. Those who had supported the system when it still had its hold on him were either dead or in nursing homes. Moreover, even when he was in his forties, revenge wouldn't have been worth it. A handful of the miscreants genuinely thought they were doing the right thing. Others went along with what seemed to be acceptable without much thought as to how he or others would be affected.

Ross included a DVD he had made in his will, outlining his thoughts on the system and how it had treated him. Then, after careful consideration, he took it out of his will, figuring it was not likely to do anyone any good in some future he wasn't a part of. Finally, he began to write it all down, his fight with the system and managed to finish it before he was too weak to continue. He told Glenda Evens to put it away somewhere and only give it to someone she thought could use it. This, she agreed to do.

He had cancer and diabetes, and he was old. Everything was closing down. He had with him, to the end, the family that the system could not prevent him from having. They cheered him up, and he tried to do the same for them. Glenda thought he was brave, but he was only sensible. He had no idea what was beyond death and hoped it would be good. He had been scared before, but wasn't anymore. Old bones are put to rest by their owner. When it came to living, someone else would take his place and possibly do a better job of fighting the system. Life deserves to be drawn to life. It was such an ancient law that the system consistently struggled with.

The nurses were good to him. They made him feel like a guest. Even so, he hated the smell of disinfectant and the odours it might be hiding. The tubes were itchy at times, but at least one of them needed to be attached to him so he could breathe more easily. He knew what remained of his hair was a mess, but he didn't care. He was bleary-eyed, but drops from the nurses helped.

Some patients talked to him about what it was like growing up in Australia in the 1970s. Two mentioned Abigail from the television show *Number 96*. Others spoke about their own experiences in so-called shag wagons. Ross would have felt bad listening to such stories if not for those two years with Glenda. As it was, he could grin and be glad for those two years.

One of the men had skin cancer but had no complaints about how he got it. He was the outdoors type and would not have given up his life as a bricklayer during the working week and surfer on the weekend for anything. "I lived my life," he told Ross. I wouldn't have been any good to anyone indoors all the time, even if it would have saved my hide."

"I saved my hide," Ross told the fellow, "But got a vitamin D deficiency and weak bones."

"No winning then?" enquired the fellow.

"No," Ross replied with a smile. "We're both here now, and I suppose that says something."

Another fellow had a bum ticker. He claimed he got it when he was younger and doing too much womanising. Neither Ross nor the other men in that ward believed that true. Even so, it was a fanciful enough conclusion, and all found it amusing.

When asked how many women he had loved, Ross said one was all he had ever needed.

"You're a lucky man," the fellow with the bum ticker told Ross.

At intervals, a preacher of one description or another floated by. Ross listened to them, never raising his hand in protest, but was still haunted by the offspring that never eventuated. Would he have made a good father? He didn't know, nor was he ever going to find out. How responsible was religion for this loss? He didn't know.

A Catholic priest brought boiled lollies to the patients who were allowed to have them and to people in the waiting room. Ross thought that was kind of him. He seemed like a good fellow. He and others were keen on Ross going upstairs rather than down. He, too, would prefer upstairs with the angels if there were stairs and pearly gates.

Were Catholic preachers still supposed to be celibate? Yes. Was this a good thing? Ross didn't think so. He found celibacy unenjoyable and, worst of all, a hindrance to understanding his fellow human beings. He had been adrift too long without a significant other. He had been cut off from humanity. This was made extremely clear in his first year with his dear lady. Catholic priests also had to feel this being cut off from the rest of existence.

Rabbis married, and Ross thought this was a good thing, too. They could undoubtedly pass on the understanding they gained from such a state to their followers. The same should have also been true of Protestant preachers. Unfortunately, it didn't seem so when it came to that one Methodist preacher he had to deal with when he was young.

Was the system a test he couldn't pass until late in life? If so, how much of it was made by Christian preachers long ago by old men who had forgotten what it was like to be young? And how did he feel so young in those two years he had been with Glenda Evens? Was that something others had also experienced?

He still believed that a God responsible for all the beauty in the world, a small percentage of which he had captured on camera, could not be so cruel as to deny him a wife earlier in life, plus children of his own. With all that begetting at the beginning of the Bible, it seemed God wanted men to be with women. The system was at fault, and behind it, there were people either trying to be religious or practical or both and, as far as he was concerned, getting it all wrong.

In his final hour, Ross found himself calling out, in his mind, to the creator of all, hoping for better things to come. He wanted to be with his lady love in Heaven, if that was at all possible when her time to leave her body came. Was that being entirely too selfish? He didn't think so.

As he slipped into unconsciousness for the last time, Ross Martin thought he saw a beautiful female angel of the Church of England variety. She beckoned to him, and he was pleased to go with her.